GREAT COMPOSERS

Piero Ventura

GREAT COMPOSERS

G. P. Putnam's Sons, New York

MARCO VENTURA created the portraits of Gregory the
Great, Guido d'Arezzo, Odo de Clugny, Desprès,
Monteverdi, Lully, Rameau, Scarlatti, Purcell, Vivaldi,
Boccherini, Bach, Handel, Gluck, Haydn, Mozart,
Paganini, Schubert, Weber, Schumann, Wagner, Brahms,
Granados, R. Strauss, and the Beatles.

ANDREA VENTURA created the portraits of Beethoven,
Berlioz, Liszt, Chopin, Rossini, Bellini, Donizetti, Verdi,
Bizet, Puccini, Tchaikovsky, Smetana, Dvořák, Albéniz,
Mahler, Debussy, Grieg, Ravel, Sibelius, Stravinsky,
Schönberg, Gershwin, Britten, Armstrong, Goodman,
Ellington.

ROBERTO PASINI collaborated on the text.

INFOLIO SNC, Verona, was the editorial collaborator.

Copyright © 1988 by Arnoldo Mondadori Editore S.p.A.,
Milan
English translation copyright © 1989 by Arnoldo
Mondadori Editore S.p.A., Milan
All rights reserved. Published simultaneously in Canada.
Originally published in Italy by Arnoldo Mondadori
Editore, 1988, under the title *Grandi Musicisti*.
English translation by Maureen Casey
Book design by Christy Hale
Printed and bound in Spain by Artes Gráficas Toledo, S.A.
D.L.TO:1489-1989
Library of Congress Cataloging-in-Publication Data

Ventura, Piero. [Grandi musicisti. English] Great composers / Piero Ventura. p.   cm.
Translation of: Grandi musicisti. Includes index.
Summary: Briefly introduces the greatest composers over
the centuries and the contributions they made to the development of music.
ISBN 0-399-21746-0
1. Composers—Juvenile literature. [1. Composers.
2. Music—History and criticism.] I. Title.
ML3929.V4613 1989 89-32861 CIP   780'.92'2—dc20

First Impression

Contents

AUTHOR'S NOTE

Great Composers is not a history of music.
It is intended as an invitation to understand
the works of the most famous musicians of
all time, in the context of the time and place
in which their talents unfolded and with an
emphasis on their artistic personalities.

These were, of course, extraordinary per-
sons, but in this book we refer to this only
occasionally, for the essential thing is to
comprehend the emotions and ideas that
these composers have succeeded in communicating by means of the most pure of all
the arts—music.

Piero Ventura

Primitive Music

Music in some form played a part in all prehistoric cultures. Primitive people believed that such sounds as the nightingale's song, the whistling wind, or the rumble of thunder were divine voices, and thus music came to play an important part in the magic and religious rites of the community.

The first wind instruments were made from large shells shaped like trumpets, while the first percussion instruments were the result of beating on hollow logs or skins stretched over empty vessels.

Yet more than just sounds, music involves organization of sounds. One sound repeated with "rhythm" creates music, a series of high or low sounds made by an instrument or voice creates a "melody," and a number of sounds all made at the same time results in "harmony." Over eons of time, these three—rhythm, melody, and harmony—have evolved from simple sounds to complex arrangements, meeting a fundamental need of the human spirit for music in every society, a need that begins for each one of us in the womb, where each moment is underlined by the rhythm of our mother's heartbeat.

Sounds are used not only to communicate but also to produce an emotional response.

The Chinese

Archaeologists have discovered traces of the presence of music in all the most ancient civilizations. Musical instruments have been found in the tombs of people who lived thousands of years ago; statuettes of musicians have emerged from excavations; and in all probability the signs on ancient papyri and stone tablets that differ from lettering are musical notations.

Music was important in China's ancient civilization. One of the oldest known Chinese instruments, a *king*, was made from stone slabs hung on a frame and struck with a mallet, while the *chin* had seven strings stretched on a split log. The *cheng*, a wind instrument, was made from a gourd. It had thirteen bamboo reeds of different lengths and when blown emitted the twelve notes of the Chinese scale. The Chinese, who also had flutes, lutes, and all sizes of bells, from very tiny ones to very large ones, often played together in groups like our modern orchestras.

Because music for the ancient Chinese was more than just a means of communicating human emotions or moods, certain instruments and notes expressed the different elements of the universe, the planets, the seasons, and the natural forces, as well as metals and colors. Confucius, who lived in 500 B.C., said, "If you want to understand a nation, listen to its music."

A king

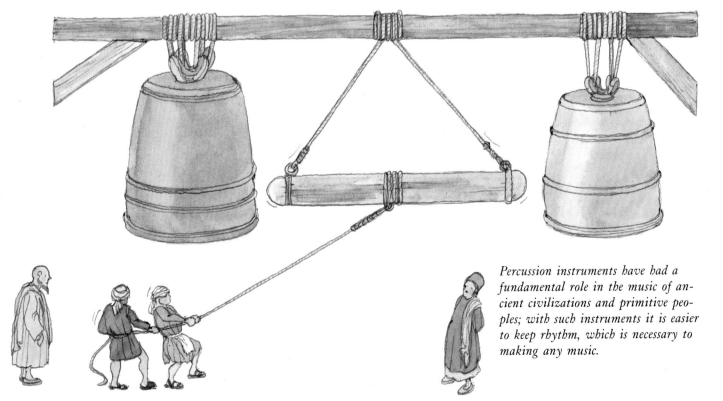

Percussion instruments have had a fundamental role in the music of ancient civilizations and primitive peoples; with such instruments it is easier to keep rhythm, which is necessary to making any music.

At right, an enormous Burmese
trumpet; below, from left to right, the
tabla, vina, and sitar, typical Indian
instruments. Dance has always been
accompanied by music, and in the
Orient this is true also for religious
rituals.

The Indians

Music in India has always accompanied all civil and religious ceremonies
as well as private and public gatherings. The many different ways that
Indians made music were called *ragas*, or "color," each color expressing
a particular mood: happy at a festival, mournful at a sad occasion, and
rhythmic for a dance. The Indians venerated music so much that the invention of certain instruments was attributed to the gods. The Indians
believed that the goddess of knowledge, Sarasvati, invented the *vina*, an
ancient stringed instrument, the *sitar*, an instrument played by plucking
chords which is still played today, and the *tabla*, which is made from a
pair of drums.

The ancient ties between music and the forces of nature, and its power
to soothe even wild animals, can be seen today in many an Indian mar-
ket, where a beggar can be found with his flute, charming a snake into
rising out of its basket.

The countries to the east of India, such as Indochina and the Malayan
Islands, also developed elaborate forms of music, often using large groups
of instruments, with the orchestras of Bali made up of percussion instruments that varied in size from tiny bells to enormous gongs.

13

The Egyptians

By 3000 B.C., music in Egypt was already well developed. Because music was considered divine, it was the concern of the priests. For many hundreds of years the Egyptians, who believed in tradition, kept in use the primitive ritual music that accompanied all the festivities of the Pharaoh's court, music composed mainly for the harp, lyre, and flute. The trumpet was also in use, especially by the armies for giving signals. In the tomb of Tutankhamen, of the eighteenth dynasty (1300 B.C.), trumpets were found that could still be played.

After the conquest of vast territories before 1000 B.C., the Egyptians blended their music with the music of the defeated countries, and it was then entrusted to groups of professional female musicians.

The people of the Middle East had cultivated sacred and festival music from prehistoric times, with the Assyrians even using music to put their soldiers in a fighting mood. The Hebrews' musical tradition began about 1000 B.C. with the 150 psalms that are attributed to King David, a harpist.

Musical groups in ancient Egypt performed with lyres, harps, lutes, and flutes.

A music lesson in Greece. In the Greek theater, dances accompanied by musical instruments were performed in the center of an outdoor auditorium. The name of this place, orchestra, *has come to mean a group of instruments or players.*

The Greeks and Romans

The ancient Greeks, who considered music important in the education of their children, believed that music had a moral significance, with certain types of music capable of strengthening the will, inspiring heroic acts, or even curing depression. The flute brightened Greek feasts, while the lyre accompanied tales of heroism and poetry (hence the word "lyrics"), with bards—singers—traveling from city to city singing heroic tales and verses of poetry.

The most celebrated was Homer, to whom the *Iliad* and *Odyssey* are attributed. Just as celebrated are the lyrical poets who dwelt on the isle of Lesbos between 700 and 600 B.C.—Alcaeus, who sang of freedom, and Sappho, who sang of love.

Music was less important to the Romans, who used it for more practical purposes, for religious functions or entertainment at festivals and banquets. The horn, which was used for military purposes, was copied by the Romans from the Germanic hordes against whom they battled for centuries.

Gregory the Great and Polyphony

When Christianity spread throughout the Roman Empire, a new kind of sacred music was born that combined Hebrew psalms and Greek hymns, but because each country had different traditions, the Catholic Church wanted to unify its music. History credits Pope Gregory the Great, pope from A.D. 590 to 604, with this achievement. The Gregorian chant, a vast collection of mostly anonymous compositions named for Pope Gregory, developed during the Middle Ages.

Over time, the Gregorian chant continued to develop, being enriched by new hymns, such as the *Dies irae* (Day of Wrath) and the *Stabat*

Pope Gregory the Great unified Christian music in the Catholic Church.

Mater (The Mother [Mary] Stood), which were attributed to great theologians such as St. Thomas Aquinas, to poets, or even to simple monks. Although the Gregorian chant has been preserved in the Benedictine monasteries to this day, the great cathedral choir schools developed "polyphony" (the study of song with more than one voice), starting from a basic Gregorian theme and then harmoniously intertwining and falling back onto the same note. The different singers and choirs had to follow their parts and at the same time sing in harmony with others. Thus was born the need to define and write on a line the height and length of each note. The evolution of the different notations at that time gave the names to the notes and musical notations of today.

Guido d'Arezzo

In western music there are two ways of naming the seven notes, both of which date back to the Middle Ages.

do (ut), re, mi, fa, sol, la, si (Italy and France)
C   D E F G A B

   The first was invented by the Benedictine monk Guido d'Arezzo. To simplify learning music for his monks, Guido called the notes by the first syllable of each hemistich (half a line of verse) in the Gregorian hymn of St. John the Baptist:

> *Ut* queant laxis   *re* sonare fibris
> *Mi* ra gestorum   *fa* muli tuorum
> *Sol* ve polluti   *la* bii reatum
> (Sancte Johannes)

   Because each hemistich of the hymn begins a grade higher than the one before it, by remembering the hymn, it was easy for the monks to intone the note written on each line. Because of his achievements, in his day Guido was considered to be almost the inventor of music.

The monk Guido d'Arezzo visited monasteries, where he taught music.

Odo de Clugny

The second method of naming the seven notes was invented by another Benedictine monk, Odo de Clugny. Odo, who was first a chorister in the church of St. Martin in Tours, in France, and then the abbot of the famous monastery of Clugny, in time was declared a saint. Odo, who established the pauses between the notes, named the notes with letters of the alphabet, beginning with "A," which corresponds to "la." Besides this, he distinguished the B flat from B natural and to this day the flat and natural are used in music.

Although secular melodies were sometimes used in religious songs, the clergy were infuriated when popular verses in Latin that were obscene or offensive were set to Gregorian melodies. These "university songs" were taken around Europe by students who were known as "wandering clerks."

Odo, a music theorist, was also abbot of the famous French monastery of Clugny.

Troubadours and the New Art

During the Middle Ages troubadours, who composed their own words and music, and minstrels, who were simply singers of songs, traveled from place to place, accompanying themselves on the lute (the forerunner of the guitar) and singing of chivalric deeds and their love of and reverence for women. Because the troubadours were close to the actual conditions of life in their time, they composed in the spoken language of the day rather than in the Latin of sacred music.

In the fourteenth century, secular music was recognized as having as much artistic value as sacred music. *Ars nova* (the new art), which originated in France, quickly spread, with the most famous troubadours making their way across Europe. The greatest representative of this school was Guillaume de Machaut, a refined poet and skilled musician who has left behind many compositions. The Florentine Francesco Landino, a blind singer who was able to play any instrument, distinguished himself in Italy.

In Italy the "new art" usually consisted of madrigals which sang of love and were written for two or more voices and based on two motives, one for the verses and one for the chorus. By that time, the viella (forerunner of the viola), flutes, horns, harps, and percussion instruments were all in use, with the organ, which was of Egyptian origin, gradually becoming the main instrument for sacred music.

In the Middle Ages, traveling troubadours and minstrels entertained the people.

Josquin Desprès

By the fifteenth century, all the great French and Flemish masters were using the polyphonic technique—that is, the study of song with more than one voice—but the result was often just a tangle of sound. While Johannes Okeghem remained the undisputed master in defining counterpoint, the scheme of the voices placed note upon note, it was his student, Josquin Desprès, who blended the voices into a fluid design, finding the major articulation while remaining faithful to diverse sentiments, and giving the music movement and great expressiveness. Martin Luther said that other masters had to do what the notes wanted, whereas the notes had to do what Josquin wanted.

With his great talent, Josquin was sought after by the most powerful courts of Europe, first in Milan, then in Rome, and finally in France. In his old age, the French court awarded Josquin a steady income.

Josquin Desprès was admired throughout Europe for his influence on music.

Konrad Paumann

Because the organ alone, or a group of instruments, could substitute for human voices, instrumental music that was free of song and words developed in the fifteenth century at a time when the organ was traditionally played by the blind. Blind from birth, Konrad Paumann was called the "wonderful blind man" by the people of Mantua, Italy, where he was organist.

Born in Nuremberg, Germany, in 1415, Paumann lived afterward at the court of Munich. He was not only an organ virtuoso but also a composer and teacher who wrote *Fundamentum organisandi*, a collection of works that established the principles and techniques of organ music.

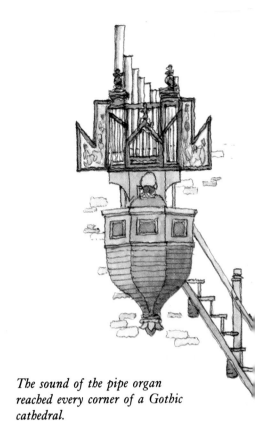

The sound of the pipe organ reached every corner of a Gothic cathedral.

The Renaissance

Polyphony reached its highest point of development and expressive capacity well into the Renaissance, that is, the sixteenth century. Every European country and every court had its own school of music called a *cappella,* directed by a *maestro.*

Orlando di Lasso, a Flemish musician who performed before half the courts of Europe, dedicating himself to both the secular madrigal and to sacred music (fifty-eight masses are attributed to him), was just as famous as Josquin Desprès.

However, in the field of sacred music the most famous composer was Pierluigi da Palestrina, who composed over one hundred masses as well as pieces for all liturgical occasions of the Church and was known everywhere as "the prince of music."

The Venetian polyphonic school had two choirs with instrumental accompaniment for its singing. In St. Mark's Cathedral there were two choir stalls with an organ and a musical group in each, with St. Mark's organist, Andrea Gabrieli, one of the first to compose solely for instruments.

In the fifteenth and sixteenth centuries in Germany, the wandering singers of the late Middle Ages became known as the *Meistersinger,* or "master singers," and established themselves in the cities, while during the Protestant Reformation in Germany, popular German songs (chorales) were adapted in order to bring the faithful into the religious fold. Reworked by great musicians, these chorales became the basis of traditional German music, both vocal and instrumental.

In the sixteenth century the most ambitious courts built elaborate theaters such as the Olympic Theater (opposite).

The English Virginals and John Dowland

As time passed, musical instruments, which began to substitute for some voices, especially the deeper ones, were played alone— as solos. The violin, which always played the melody, was introduced in the sixteenth century, with the harpsichord, a new keyboard instrument that interwove harmonious chords. Other stringed keyboard instruments—the clavichord, the spinet, and the virginal—were the forerunners of the harpsichord. The virginal, with its light and refined sound, was common in England and is said to have been named in homage to Queen Elizabeth I, the Virgin Queen, to whom the English colonists had already dedicated the colony of Virginia. However, this instrument probably existed before the reign of Elizabeth and may have acquired its

During the Elizabethan period, the English nobility made the countryside a setting for their plays and music.

name because it was part of the musical education of young ladies of the English upper classes. Whatever the origin of the term, a large school of "virginalists" (musicians who composed for the instrument) certainly flourished in England during Elizabeth's reign.

The lute, which accompanied secular music, was also used as a solo instrument to play airs arranged in suites (different pieces played in succession). The Englishman John Dowland was a great composer and virtuoso who was famous for his lute playing throughout Europe and whose "heavenly touch enraptured the human senses." Dowland, who had lived in Paris, at the Danish court, and had visited Italy, was appointed to the court of King James I, where he served until his death in 1626.

Claudio Monteverdi

*Performances in squares and churches
in the seventeenth century developed
into public theaters.*

28

In the sixteenth century, secular music began to use one voice accompanied by an instrumental group in place of many voices. At the same time, "drama for music," called *melodramma*, was developing, as well as "opera" in which actor-singers played and sang different parts. These changes matured in the seventeenth century under Claudio Monteverdi, who is considered to be the creator of the opera. Monteverdi, originally a viola player, was choirmaster at the court of the Gonzagas in Mantua, Italy. He was called to Venice in 1612 as music director of St. Mark's Cathedral, where he remained until his death in 1643, dedicating himself to madrigals, of which he published five books, sacred music, and opera—primarily vocal music.

Although previously only court theaters had existed, now public theaters were opening where anyone could attend for a fee. Preferring historical characters and comical situations, audiences also loved spectacular stage effects. And Monteverdi, who liked the dramatic theater and opera best, was the man to satisfy their tastes, composing *Orfeo* and *Arianna* in Mantua and *L'incoronazione di Poppea* (The Coronation of Poppea) in Venice.

Jean-Philippe Rameau

Jean-Baptiste Lully

Jean-Baptiste Lully and Jean-Philippe Rameau

Musical theater developed in France under the leadership of Giovanni Battista Lulli, an Italian, who as a talented violinist and dancer had gone to France as a young boy where he was known as Jean-Baptiste Lully. "Court ballets" were popular under King Louis XIV, but because the plots were weak, dialogue and sung parts were introduced between the ballets until they became true and proper musical dramas. Lully col-

laborated with the great French playwrights Molière, Corneille, and Racine to produce comedies and dramas of which *Armide* was his masterpiece. Lully, who also wrote instrumental works, was the first to introduce an opera with an "overture," or opening symphony.

Meanwhile, Italian opera, which was flourishing, became famous all over Europe. Especially popular were "comic" operas based on amusing situations with entertaining characters in which the singers could display their musical ability.

The Frenchman Jean-Philippe Rameau was the most important figure in French music during the eighteenth century. As composer for the "chamber" of King Louis XV, Rameau who was an expert on musical instruments, introduced large orchestral pieces into operas with great success.

French opera in the seventeenth century was greatly influenced by Jean-Baptiste Lully and Jean-Philippe Rameau.

Alessandro Scarlatti

Alessandro Scarlatti was a much sought-after musician throughout Italy.

During the seventeenth century, musical theater in Italy consisted of three schools: those of Venice, Rome, and Naples. The historical and comic operas of Venice were based on simple continuous melodies and spectacular stagecraft. Rome's musical theater, influenced by the oratorio, centered around Biblical themes and was performed without scenery in churches or religious surroundings, while in Naples, the carelessly put-together popular operas were based mainly on airs with little thought to plot.

Alessandro Scarlatti, with his extraordinary musical talent, imposed a stricter form on the operas of Naples, sustaining the plot with vigorous compositions. Because he could adapt to the musical style of each city, he helped to unify Italian opera. With many musicians following his example, Italian opera soon conquered all of Europe.

In addition, because of their instrumental compositions, Scarlatti and his son Domenico attracted the attention of many great contemporary musicians who were more interested in studying pure harmony than in the opera.

Henry Purcell

Henry Purcell, who died at the age of thirty-six, dedicated only his last six years to opera. He was the major English composer of the seventeenth century. Using instruments and songs to produce purely entertaining music, Purcell wasn't particularly interested in the social and political problems of his day. Nevertheless, he wrote the *Welcome Songs* for the return of the English king to London, in addition to a hymn for the coronation of James II, earning him the title of "the genius of the Restoration," that period in England that saw the return of the monarchy after the revolution led by Oliver Cromwell.

Purcell's operatic masterpiece was Dido and Aeneas, *taken from Virgil's* Aeneid. *His stage music for* The Fairy Queen, *based on Shakespeare's* Midsummer Night's Dream, *is also very beautiful.*

Antonio Vivaldi

The concerto—the grouping together of a number of instruments—was perfected by Antonio Vivaldi, who produced compositions written for all the principal instruments of the day except the harpsichord. The concerto differed from the "concertino," which consisted of a few especially skillful players, and from the "concerto grosso," which utilized the entire orchestra. When a composition was dedicated to one instrument, or to no more than three, it was called a "sonata."

Among Vivaldi's most well-known works are his four concertos called *The Four Seasons, The Night, The Hunt,* and the *Storm at Sea.* Vivaldi's

The Venice of Antonio Vivaldi's day was a rich and fascinating city.

first two collections of concertos, which made him famous throughout Europe, were studied by the foremost composers of that time, including Bach.

The Venice of Vivaldi's day was rich, pleasure-loving, capricious and decaying. With its theaters, and its carnival that lasted for weeks, it continuously demanded new music. Gifted composers such as Tommaso Albinoni and Benedetto Marcello—and especially Vivaldi—were kept at work furnishing fresh scores. Wealthy families organized extravagant parties in their palaces along the Grand Canal or in their villas on the mainland, and they were attended by princes from all the royal houses of Europe. They went mad over music. The Grimanis, for example, employed only servants who could sing or play music!

Vivaldi, however, composed the major part of his works for a Venetian conservatory where female orphans or outcast girls were taken in and given a musical education. Under the guidance of the Master, these anonymous young artists studied with passion and performed in a public concert every Sunday. They were hidden behind a grille, perhaps, it is speculated, because some of the students were deformed.

Vivaldi's inventiveness seemed inexhaustible, and his melodies caught on immediately because they were spontaneous and lively. While his "allegri" are full of color and energy, the "adagi" can transport one into a state of dream-like enchantment.

Acting as his own manager, Vivaldi traveled often to Prague, Vienna, and Amsterdam to conduct his works as well as to oversee the printing of his scores.

Luigi Boccherini

The eighteenth century produced much gracious, charming music, such as the playing of stringed instruments in the elegant salons of aristocrats by small groups (a trio, a quartet, or a quintet). These concerts were called *chamber music.*

The first known permanent string quartet consisted of four Italian musicians, including Luigi Boccherini, who was not only a virtuoso on the violoncello, but was also one of the best-known composers of chamber music. After his success throughout Europe as a young concert player, Boccherini spent the rest of his life in Madrid, playing and composing music for Spain's aristocracy. Although his larger works featured stringed instruments, they also included the guitar and the pianoforte, which had appeared about 1709 but which initially had not made much of an impression on either musicians or public.

Luigi Boccherini composed chamber music for the aristocracy of eighteenth-century Madrid. Gentlemen, always in wig and ruff, courted the ladies in the salons between one concerto and another.

The marketplace in Eisenach, Saxony, where Bach was born and raised.

Johann Sebastian Bach

Although much of music is experimentation, with every successful effort imitated and followed, it was Johann Sebastian Bach who summarized and unified musical language. By showing *how* to make music through his works, Bach's genius was not in inventing new musical forms but in showing what could be done with existing forms using illustrations of all possible combinations, passages, and forms of expression.

Bach, who came from a family of musicians, was a singer, organist, and violinist in various German churches and courts before settling permanently in Leipzig, where he was a composer and director of musical events. Unlike most other musicians, Bach preferred the security of a government job which allowed him to enjoy a normal family life as well as time to compose music both for himself and professionally. Bach was a deeply religious man. He had two wives and twenty children, ten of whom survived and became musicians.

Transcending the often superficial and empty music of the eighteenth century as well as the somewhat dry Protestant sacred music, Bach produced religious music of incredible force and depth, such as the *Passion According to St. John* and the *Passion According to St. Matthew*—works that interpreted and communicated the mysteries of faith.

37

Although his children called him "old fogey" and his contemporaries often found him old-fashioned and boring, today Bach's music is heard throughout the world.

At Potsdam in 1737, the King of Prussia suggested a theme to Bach, who executed a series of improvisations later arranged in the Musical Offering.

Out of Bach's study of Italian instrumental music, especially Vivaldi's, came many concertos and sonatas, among them the six *Brandenburg Concertos.* Believing that music students should also learn to appreciate the aesthetic and moral values of music, Bach wrote *The Well-Tempered Clavier,* a collection of compositions for the teaching of music which defined *tonality* in a poetic way.

Bach also wrote simple exercises for his wife and children which he collected into *Libretti* for the keyboard. His magnificent *Goldberg Variations,* written for a lady of that name who suffered from insomnia, included some thirty elaborations on the same theme and touch every sensation. In *The Art of the Fugue* Bach demonstrated how to extract all possible combinations from a theme as well as revealing his secrets as a musician, his legacy to posterity.

Georg Frideric Handel

Like his contemporary and fellow Saxon, Bach, Georg Frideric Handel initially disliked Italian opera. However, after traveling to Italy and meeting Vivaldi, Scarlatti, and other important musicians, he began to appreciate and to write operas. Invited to England, where no new opera composers had taken the place left by Purcell, Handel enjoyed a period of great success despite hostility from the king and some of the court. Because his instrumental music was never well received in England, Handel continued to write operas, although English society never really accepted these extravagant spectacles performed in a foreign language by temperamental singers.

Handel then turned to the oratorio, which preserved the dramatic spirit of his music and also used the English language. His masterpieces are often performed today: for example, *Israel in Egypt*, *Jephtha*, and especially the *Messiah*.

Handel composed the "Water Music" in honor of a trip on the Thames River taken by the English royal court.

40

Italian Opera

Audiences in eighteenth-century Italy, as elsewhere in Europe, preferred opera, with its poetry, music, dancing, and dramatic staging, to instrumental music. Opera, which combined action, characterization, and emotion in the *libretto* (the poetic text), became less abstract and more descriptive, and thus more easily understood.

In *serious opera*, as opposed to *comic opera*, the librettist Pietro Metastasio, using elegant language as well as recitative and final arias to give the characters psychological depth, employed a chorus to enhance emotions, and dances to complement the plot. In *comic opera*, the great Venetian playwright Carlo Goldoni introduced nonstop comic situations and exciting action, with his characters stating their point of view at the end of each act.

Because the audience often demanded selections taken from different operas as well as dances taken out of context, operatic muddles sometimes resulted. In addition, temperamental singers, exercising "artistic freedom," sometimes didn't even bother to complete their arias, and occasionally came to blows on the stage. Eighteenth-century Italian opera was soon imitated throughout Europe, with composers nearly always setting Italian librettos to music so that with Italian the common language, there was little difference between German opera presented in London and Italian opera performed in Paris.

It wasn't until Pergolesi's comic opera *La serva padrona* (The Maid as Mistress) was presented in Paris that Italian opera succeeded in France. The French intellectuals, who advocated social reform, liked Italian opera with its themes of the family and social classes, and especially its satires of the aristocracy. Naturally, censorship resulted, so that more than one musician tangled with the law.

With artists such as Italians Giovanni Paisiello and Domenico Cimarosa, and geniuses such as Austrians Haydn and Mozart composing, Italian-style opera prevailed until the end of the eighteenth century. Although new trends in the beginning of the nineteenth century introduced the Romantic era, the influence of classical Italian opera nonetheless remained dominant throughout Europe.

The most important Italian opera theaters, many of which are still in use today, were built in the eighteenth century. The large halls, with their seats removed, also served as ballrooms for the nobility.

Christoph Willibald Gluck

Although Christoph Willibald Gluck was
born in Bohemia (now Czechoslovakia), he
worked mainly in Vienna and Paris. He
composed over thirty operas in the Italian
style while in Milan—works that made him
famous throughout Europe. In Vienna,
Gluck worked with the famous librettist and
poet Ranieri de Calzabigi reforming the
structure of opera. Because he believed too
much emphasis was being placed on melody
and on the singers' prowess rather than on
the plot, Gluck sought more unity between
music and action. He also believed that the
overture should truly introduce the opera
rather than just function as an instrumental
composition for the entertainment of the
waiting audience.

The opera Orpheus and Eurydice *by Gluck was based on a Greek myth about the musician Orpheus.*

Although Gluck took his new ideas to Paris, Italian opera had become so popular there that he aroused immediate controversy, with his last opera, *Echo and Narcissus,* failing so badly in 1779 that he retired to Vienna and stopped composing.

Although his ideas on the structure of the opera were not followed immediately, later they became important to musical artists in different cultural climates. Some of Gluck's operas are still performed, the most famous of which is *Orpheus and Eurydice,* an interpretation of a Greek myth. Some of his works preceding his "reform" have not been forgotten either.

Paris and Vienna were the most important cities for Gluck's career, but Milan and London formed him artistically. In the English capital (shown here), where he lived in 1745 and 1746, he often met Handel.

On this street in Eisenstadt is
the first house Franz Joseph
Haydn bought while serving
the Esterházy princes. Haydn
is considered the father of the
symphony; though the musical
form existed already, he developed it to perfection.

Franz Joseph Haydn

At the end of the eighteenth century, Vienna was not only the capital of a great power that included Austria, Bohemia, Hungary, and the Lombard-Venetian area, but also the musical capital of Europe. Because the cultural interests of the Austro-Hungarian nobility centered on music, they held private concerts in their residences and public concerts to raise money for charities.

Franz Joseph Haydn spent a productive thirty years with the Princes Paul and Nikolaus Esterházy on their Hungarian estate. There he composed over one hundred symphonies, dozens of concertos for string quartets, and sonatas for piano and other instruments, as well as operas based on the librettos of Carlo Goldoni.

Haydn originated a symphonic style that prevailed up to the twentieth century. His music, like the other arts of his era, is defined by the term "classicism." Previously the symphony had served merely as an opening piece for an opera, but under Haydn the structure of the symphony was carefully defined and arranged. From that point on, the symphony acquired a life of its own, opening up enormous possibilities for future composers.

Wolfgang Amadeus Mozart

When the young musical genius Wolfgang Amadeus Mozart was only four or five years old, his ambitious father, Leopold, took him on concert tours throughout Europe where he astounded his audiences. In 1781, young Mozart, expelled from his position with the Archbishop of Salzburg, traveled to Vienna to try his fortunes there. His father, who never understood his son's longing for independence or the musical volcano in his soul, was eager for Wolfgang to find a dignified position which would put his extraordinary talents to use. Mozart, who worked frantically in Vienna to maintain his boyhood fame, always remained somewhat childlike; his music expresses a vein of playfulness and mischief. As the most "pleasing" music ever written, Mozart's works tickle the senses even while reaching the highest peaks of excellence.

Mozart's house in Salzburg. His father, Leopold, was very strict with the little genius. In Vienna Mozart lived in a modest house and faced frequent financial difficulties. He was the target of other musicians' envy, and it is said that Antonio Salieri, the imperial choirmaster, poisoned him.

Mozart's difficult years in Vienna were also his most productive, when he wrote his greatest masterpieces, the operas *Don Giovanni* and *The Magic Flute*, the *Jupiter* symphony, the Quintet in G Minor, the nocturnal serenade *A Little Night Music*, and many others, with his last great work—the *Requiem*—composed as death approached. In December 1791 Mozart died at the age of thirty-five.

Mozart, who began composing when he was eleven, knew how to capture emotion better than any other musician. Although he dedicated himself to various types of music, and worked within the musical forms of his time, his mature music was nonetheless original and free. Neither a reformer nor an innovator, Mozart summarized the past and brought it to perfection, while at the same time he opened up new paths for the future, and in so doing created music that is eternal.

The young Mozart traveled all over Europe giving concerts.

When audiences clamored for an encore, Paganini replied, "Paganini does not repeat."

Niccolò Paganini

At the beginning of the nineteenth century, while the pianoforte was striving to become the undisputed king of Romantic music, the violin was reaching its highest peak of virtuosity. And master of the violin was Niccolò Paganini, in whose hands the instrument could release a brilliance of sound that could produce absolutely astonishing effects. Because the classical compositions were inadequate for Paganini's fiery technique and inexhaustible imagination, he began to compose his own works, mostly variations on the themes of famous musicians.

Typical of the Romantic figures of his time, Paganini remained so surrounded by mystery that legends quickly developed around him. A reckless adventurer and opportunist, Paganini embodied the genius who was intolerant of all rules and answerable only to himself.

Ludwig van Beethoven

Born in Bonn, Germany, Ludwig van Beethoven, who barely earned enough to survive for ten years in Vienna by giving piano concerts, had all his compositions printed in the hopes that one day he could live on the royalties. In 1789, the French Revolution, with its affirmation of the artist's right to express himself freely, was a strong influence on Beethoven's music. Because classical forms were narrow and the tempos too restrictive, in the hands of thirty-year-old Beethoven the sonata and the traditional symphony were swept away, and the most intimate feelings and emotions were expressed passionately as the musician bared his soul. By molding the musical language to meet his own needs, Beethoven was the forerunner of the music of the Romantic era.

Unfortunately, when Beethoven was thirty-two, his hearing began to deteriorate until he eventually became totally deaf. After a period of despair, when he even considered suicide, Beethoven found the strength to devote his life to the music which he could now only *feel* within himself. Always somewhat isolated from the outside world by his morose and distrustful nature, Beethoven became completely alienated from society by his deafness. His last performance in public was in 1815, when he played his Concerto for Piano No. 5 before the crowned heads of Europe who were in Vienna to restore the old monarchies after Napoleon's defeat.

Beethoven, while composing, gave piano concerts to earn a living.

Although Beethoven had dedicated his Third Symphony, the *Eroica,* to Napoleon, who seemed to symbolize liberty and fraternity, when Napoleon betrayed the cause of freedom by being crowned Emperor, Beethoven ripped up the dedication.

Although the Romantic generation that followed Beethoven mythologized him by picturing him as a heroic artist who fought against social conventions, injustice, and hypocrisy, Beethoven was far more than that, and his greatness was fully recognized only after his death. The progressive development of Beethoven's brilliant compositions signaled the beginning of a new era in all fields of human creativity and experience.

Beethoven's house in Heiligenstadt was close to Vienna but still enabled him to stay in contact with the countryside, where he loved to take long walks. It was here that he realized he was going deaf when he could no longer hear the bells in the nearby church tower.

Franz Schubert

Although Franz Schubert, who was born in Vienna just a few years after the death of Mozart, was for a while a teacher like his father, a generous friend took the young Franz into his home and convinced him to dedicate his life to music. Schubert, who composed piano melodies that he presented to friends who played music together in their homes, wrote more than three hundred sonatas for trios, quartets, and quintets, as well as over six hundred songs called *Lieder*. Schubert also composed symphonies, two of which, the "Great" and the "Unfinished," were performed after his tragic death in 1828 at the age of thirty-one.

Schubert's music, especially the chamber compositions such as the sonatas, was as warm, intimate, and friendly as those private musical evenings with friends that became known as "Schubertiads."

Franz Schubert always lived in financial straits and in poor environments, except when he was the guest of friends or the teacher of the Esterházy princesses.

Carl Maria von Weber

Until the nineteenth century, the official language of opera was Italian, but with the development of national opera theaters, the language, subject matter, and music of operas were drawn from the heritage and traditions of each country.

The composer Carl Maria von Weber, famous for his brilliant concertos, established German national opera on a firm foundation. His *Freischütz*, a typical German Romantic story, gloomy and magical, contained elements of pure love, all dominated by the force of nature. The call of the horn, the lament of the clarinet, the chorus of hunters, which all evoke the mystery of the forest, serve to clarify the *leitmotiv*—the principal musical theme of the opera.

Weber is also known for his brilliant concertos, for his orchestral works such as *Aufforderung zum Tanz* (Invitation to the Dance), and for his operas *Oberon* and *Euryanthe*.

Weber came from a theatrical family who traveled around Germany. He began to insert themes (leitmotivs) into his operas, an invention which Wagner later exploited.

Felix Mendelssohn-Bartholdy

Mendelssohn was inspired by sunny Italy to write his Fourth Symphony, called the Italian. *He said, "It is the gayest work I have ever written."*

Happy by nature, Felix Mendelssohn-Bartholdy was born in 1809 into a cultured, wealthy German family which encouraged his interests in painting, literature, and music. At the age of seventeen young Felix wrote the famous "Wedding March" for *A Midsummer Night's Dream* which has since been played at weddings all over the world.

Mendelssohn, whose career skyrocketed, appreciated the classics of the immediate past, such as Haydn's and Mozart's works, as well as the music of Bach and Handel. Mendelssohn rediscovered Bach, reviving the *Passion According to St. Matthew* in 1829, one hundred years after Bach had written it.

Although Mendelssohn was also a Romantic, he lacked the sense of conflict and the stormy passions of most of the Romantic composers, and his balanced and serene character is especially evident in his five symphonies. Charmed as Mendelssohn's life seemed to be, he died at the height of his career of a cerebral hemorrhage. He was thirty-eight.

At Weimar, Franz Liszt, a great admirer of Hector Berlioz, organized a festival for his friend's music. But Schumann wrote of Berlioz, "It is hard to say if he is a genius or an adventurer of music."

Hector Berlioz

Hector Berlioz was one of the most Romantic personalities of the nineteenth century. Although he was French, he was more successful in Romantic Germany than he was in the more moderate climate of France. The *Symphonie fantastique,* which brought him fame in 1830 and became a cornerstone of music to come, describes, in traditional form, terrible dreams and violent passions, ending in a symphonic poem. This work makes effective use of the *leitmotiv,* the "leading motive."

Berlioz was strongly attracted to opera, but because he liked colossal spectaculars over which his powerful orchestration would triumph, his first opera, *Benvenuto Cellini,* failed miserably. And his next opera was so long that he had to cut it in half to make it acceptable to an audience. Nevertheless, in 1855 he presented the kind of spectacular he preferred when nine hundred voices performed his *Te Deum.*

Franz Liszt

The true apostle of Romanticism was Franz Liszt, who first performed on the piano at the age of eight and packed all the concert halls of Europe with his piano virtuosity when he was older. Crossed hands, mad runs on the keyboard, and plucked chords were used (and often invented) by Liszt. Some of his piano compositions were possible for only the most expert player.

Because some of his melodies were sentimental while others were macabre and violent, Liszt was often accused of being either superficial or melodramatic. Even though Liszt's compositions broke with the classical forms, they had an architecture that sustained them. They were based, not on harmonic variations on a specific theme, but on the continual transformation of the theme, which constantly redefined itself, found other ways to express itself, forming the melodic continuum that is the most conspicuous feature of Romantic music.

Franz Liszt was always warmly applauded by his faithful public.

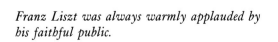

Fryderyk Chopin

Although Fryderyk Chopin was an exile from Poland living in France during revolutionary times, he was introverted and non-political. Called the "poet of music" because he revealed his most intimate self in his music, Chopin transposed passionate feeling into short and elegant compositions that were spontaneous, new, and completely original. The Preludes and Nocturnes display Chopin's lyrical talents, while the Mazurkas and Polonaises, which were typical Polish dances, express his love for his native land.

Chopin, who was also a Romantic in his personal life, was famous for his relationship with the authoress George Sand, with whom he lived on Majorca. Although she nursed him through a long period of illness, Chopin died of tuberculosis in 1849 at the age of thirty-eight. Mozart's *Requiem* was played at his funeral in Paris.

Although Chopin left Poland forever, he never forgot his homeland.

Richard Wagner

Born in Leipzig, Germany, in 1813, Richard Wagner saw in music a means to communicate his ideas in a combination of words, notes, and dramatic expression. As a young man, he envisioned a "drama for music" that would express the German soul and assert the cultural role of that nation.

In 1848–49, when Wagner became involved in the revolutionary movement against the aristocracy and was wanted by the police for terrorism, he fled Germany for Switzerland. His meeting with the revolutionary, Romantic poet Heinrich Heine resulted in his first two significant works, the operas *Der fliegende Holländer* (The Flying Dutchman) and *Tannhäuser*. During his long exile, he sketched a cycle of four operas (a tetralogy) based on ancient Nordic mythology. He called it *Der Ring des Nibelungen*. This immense masterpiece was interrupted by two other operas, *Die Meistersinger von Nürnberg* and *Tristan und Isolde*, but eventually became a reality through the support of "mad" King Ludwig II of Bavaria, whose devotion to Wagner never faltered and whose support cost him his throne and his life.

The Walküre *Brünnhilde tells Siegmund that death is near—the gods have spoken. She will then try to rescue him, for which she will be punished. Ancient Germanic mythology has entered the opera.*

Wagner's operas took a long time to be accepted outside of Germany, primarily because he rejected accepted musical forms, something begun by the early Romantics such as Weber. In Wagner's music, an "infinite" melody constantly renews itself, with themes emerging, intertwining, disappearing, and re-emerging. Because Wagner seems to carry dissonance to the limits of endurance, hearing one of his operas can be to some breathtaking, while others find it unbearable.

The immense size and complex staging of Wagner's operas called for construction of an appropriate theater. Through a public subscription and the generous aid of King Ludwig II of Bavaria, the new theater was inaugurated in Bayreuth in 1876 and quickly became the temple of German opera.

Robert Schumann

Robert Schumann abandoned law as a young man to take up music, but injured his right hand so badly that his promising career as a pianist was interrupted. His wife, Clara, the daughter of his piano teacher, not only played his compositions for him but also helped him organize his many projects as a composer, music critic, and founder of a musical journal. Schumann strongly believed in musical education and founded a review in which he followed with great care all the developments of the music of his time.

Overwork, little success as a composer, and emotional instability caused Schumann to suffer a mental breakdown. While director of the Düsseldorf symphony orchestra, he experienced hallucinations and threw himself into the Rhine. Although his life was saved, in 1854 he consented to be committed to an asylum where he died two years later. His best-remembered works are for the piano, among them *Scenes from Childhood* and *Album for the Young,* two collections of pieces for piano study that he would have tried out on his seven children.

Because Schumann injured his hand as a young man, he was unable to continue his career as a virtuoso pianist.

As an old man, Brahms appeared in public only to conduct his own works.

Johannes Brahms

Introduced to music early, young Johannes Brahms earned his living by playing in Hamburg tavern orchestras. By twenty he was accompanying celebrated soloists on the piano. Brahms, who got along well with Schumann, befriended Clara Schumann at the time of her husband's illness and death.

Brahms was accused of being an academic tied to the past, and public performances of his works caused controversy in Germany. So Brahms, a northerner and fervent Protestant who was rather averse to high society, found a new home in Vienna. An admirer of Beethoven, Brahms was over forty when he presented his First Symphony, which was sarcastically dubbed "The Tenth" in reference to Beethoven's Ninth. Brahms's friend Hans von Bülow, the famous conductor, was responsible for making Brahms's music known and appreciated throughout Europe. With Wagner's death in 1883, Brahms became Germany's most famous composer.

The Rhine, Europe's most "romantic" river, and the scene of countless bloody battles, has been the inspiration for many musical works.

Finale of an act from Rossini's opera The Barber of Seville. *It is an exhilarating moment, when all the characters come onstage and give their view of the situation.*

Gioacchino Rossini

Known as the "last of the classicists," Gioacchino Rossini, who was born into a musical family, distanced himself from the Romantic attitudes of his day. At eighteen, he made his debut in Venice with *La cambiale di matrimonio* (The Bill of Marriage). There followed a series of operas for La Fenice in Venice and La Scala in Milan, until he was offered a contract in

Naples, where his *Elisabetta regina a'Inghilterra* (Elizabeth, Queen of England) played to a packed audience in the San Carlo theater. There followed successes in Vienna, London, and Paris. Because of his rather sullen conservatism, the Romanticists hated him, although he was neither greedy nor insensitive as they charged. To prove that he could write Romantic opera, Rossini presented *William Tell,* after which he retired to compose only for himself.

During his Paris retirement he worked to smooth the way for the international success of other emerging Italian musicians—Bellini, Donizetti, and Verdi.

Not only are Rossini's masterpieces *The Barber of Seville* and *L'Italiana in Algeri* (The Italian Girl in Algiers) being produced today, but so are many of his other operas, both serious and comic.

Vincenzo Bellini and Gaetano Donizetti

A keen rivalry existed between two young and talented composers of opera, the blond Bellini and the swarthy Donizetti.

During the nineteenth century, two talented young musicians—Vincenzo Bellini from southern Italy and Gaetano Donizetti from northern Italy—competed for the hearts of opera audiences. Although there was no real hostility, there was such rivalry between them that they were both driven to continuously have an opera in production.

Because the music of Bellini and Donizetti was as different as their personalities, the public's loyalties were divided. The poetic vein in Bellini, who embodied the ideal of Italian Romanticism, was evident in his crystal-clear, tender, and emotional melodies, while Donizetti was more concerned with drama, complex orchestration, and the rhythm of events.

For ten years after the death of Bellini in 1835 at the age of thirty-four, Donizetti was the undisputed master of Italian opera. His operas were a showcase for unhappy, lovelorn heroines—*Anna Bolena, Maria Stuarda,* and *Lucia di Lammermoor*—with the clash between heart and head the theme, as always in Italian Romanticism.

Giuseppe Verdi

Giuseppe Verdi wrote six operas during the 1840s expressing his commitment to the Italian revolutionary movement of that time. With the defeat of the movement in 1848 and 1849, Verdi's less heroic operas written in the 1850s—*Rigoletto, Il trovatore,* and *La traviata*—were a disappointment to those who expected his usual patriotic themes.

Verdi, who came from a humble Italian family, lost his young wife and two small children. There followed a period of intense work that he called "the prison years." Finally attaining fame and wealth, he bought an estate in his old home region of Sant'Agata for himself and his second wife, the singer Giuseppina Strepponi.

Verdi's reputation grew as he composed masterpieces such as *Don Carlos,* performed in Paris, and *Aida,* which was commissioned by Egypt in 1871 for the opening of the Suez Canal. In the isolation of his estate, Verdi composed his majestic *Requiem,* reappearing on the opera scene again in 1887 with *Otello* and in 1893 with the joyous *Falstaff,* a fitting conclusion to his development as a composer.

Today, Verdi is the composer with the most operas in the repertoires of the world's musical theaters. His fame was guaranteed when he triumphed at Milan's La Scala, which was the most prestigious opera house in the world. La Scala was built in 1778 on the site of the ancient church Santa Maria della Scala. Bombed during World War II, it was quickly restored as a symbol of the city. The new building was inaugurated in 1946 by a concert conducted by Arturo Toscanini.

French Opera

The Academy of Music in Paris—the Opéra—which was central to the French musical world of the nineteenth century, was attended mostly by the upper middle classes. Because the theater was financed by the Ministry of Culture, it conveyed government propaganda, first for the restoration of the monarchy and then for the establishment of the Second Empire under Napoleon III.

The operatic spectaculars, with their drama, impressive scenery, and huge crowd scenes with coronations, battles, and processions, were called "grand opera," as opposed to the old comic operas. Because of the strong nationalism of that time, Italian composers such as Verdi were greatly influenced by grand opera.

The Paris Théâtre Lyrique, which was less official and therefore less

restrictive, was the center of courageously modern music and culture throughout the second half of the nineteenth century. Fortunately, the really great musicians such as Gounod, Massenet, and Bizet composed for all the theaters. Gounod, who was torn between a religious calling and his music, wrote many sacred compositions as a young man in Rome, followed by a long period in which he wrote operatic master-pieces such as *Faust* and *Roméo et Juliette* as well as his famous *Ave Maria*.

Jules Massenet won the honored Grand Prix de Rome, composing his first operas in Rome, with his masterpieces *Manon* and *Werther* proving that French national opera could also be successful outside of France. Camille Saint-Saëns was also responsible for this diffusion and left behind many important instrumental compositions, as well as fifteen operas including *Samson and Delilah*, which is still in repertoires today.

In 1865 Paris got its own opera house, called simply the Opéra, designed by Charles Garnier. The magnificence and richness of the decoration both outside and inside give an idea of the importance and prestige the opera house could bring to any nineteenth-century city.

Georges Bizet

French opera's real innovator and genius was Georges Bizet who, with his opera *Carmen* swept away the academic excesses of grand opera, the wooden stereotypes of comic opera, and operatic sentimentality in general. Bizet's lively scenes, flowing with brilliant rhythm, contribute to the opera's unity and strength.

Because of its realistic characters and emotions, when *Carmen* was presented at the Opéra-Comique theater, it created an immediate scandal. Bizet, who never had confidence in his own ability and was often depressed, died in desperation a few days after the opening. Only six months later *Carmen*, the masterpiece of French opera, triumphed in Vienna.

Carmen dances on the table in the second act of Bizet's opera.

Giacomo Puccini

Born in Lucca, Italy, Giacomo Puccini studied as a young man at the Milan Conservatory, where he lived in a rented room with his cousin, thus providing the setting for his most famous opera, *La Bohème*.

After the deaths of Verdi and Wagner, European opera composers tried to reject Romanticism by imitating the realistic literature of the day. Puccini was part of this trend, although his music had more depth, and he knew how to interpret the changes that were going on. Although he loved his Tuscan home, he never lost contact with the world, and two of his operas, *La fanciulla del West* (The Girl of the Golden West) and *Il trittico* (a triptych, or three operas), made their debuts in New York. Puccini's operas *Turandot*, set in China, and *Madama Butterfly*, set in Japan, provided exotic settings which he enriched with unusual harmonies and sounds.

Puccini died before he finished Turandot, *his opera set in ancient China. When, at La Scala, on April 25, 1924, Maestro Toscanini conducted the first performance, he halted respectfully at the point where Puccini had to leave off.*

French and Austrian Operetta

Developed in the second half of the nineteenth century and lasting until the 1930s, the operetta, which was derived from comic opera, was a very happy form of musical theater that was part song and part recitation. Operettas, which were often set in a fantasy world, proposed carefree entertainment in the form of comical and satirical stories aimed at the high society which came to see them.

In France, the operetta's success during the Second Empire was due to the witty Jacques Offenbach, who composed a hundred operettas. In 1870, after France's humiliating defeat by Prussia, the French operetta turned from satirizing militarism and nationalism to lighter, safer subjects. Offenbach, who was also a success in Vienna, was immediately imitated by the Viennese composer Johann Strauss, the Hungarian

Operetta, like the comic opera from which it is derived, was based on standard, predictable plots. Happy endings were obligatory, and exotic settings common. Often the basic plot of operetta is nothing but a simple rescue story.

Women in crinoline, men in full uniform, immense balls with gilt moldings, crystal chandeliers: carefree Hapsburg society amuses itself in turn-of-the-century Vienna. The music, of course, was provided by Johann Strauss.

Emmerich Kálmán, and the Bohemian Franz Lehár, whose *Merry Widow* is perhaps the most famous operetta today. Rarely satirical, Viennese operetta was an enjoyable spectacle of songs and waltzes.

With *Die Fledermaus* (The Bat), Johann Strauss, known as the Waltz King, began a productive ten years presenting operettas, although his most frequently performed works are his waltzes such as "On the Beautiful Blue Danube," which symbolizes Viennese charm.

Operetta caught on in Italy at the beginning of the twentieth century, while in England, Arthur Sullivan and Sidney Jones produced operettas from which American musical comedy and musical films are derived.

Pyotr Ilyich Tchaikovsky

Tchaikovsky's symphonic ballet
Swan Lake *is enjoyed by*
audiences around the world.

Pyotr Ilyich Tchaikovsky, the most famous Russian musician recognized outside Russia, was attracted to European Romantic music because it expressed the personal sentiments of the artist. During trips to Europe and America, he assisted at the productions of French, German, and Italian musicians, learning from each. Although Tchaikovsky, who was introduced to music by his mother, who died when he was fifteen, was a lawyer, he couldn't stay away from music for long. He took a position at the Conservatory in Moscow, where his cosmopolitan music was admired, and a rich widow, whom he never met, paid him a salary so that he could devote all his time to composing. Technically elegant, Tchaikovsky's music is bright—almost dazzling—on the surface, but contains an underlying melancholy that reflects the composer's pessimism. Two of his best operas, *The Queen of Spades* and *Eugene Onegin*, for example, contain characters who are victims of fate.

Tchaikovsky was the originator of a new style, the symphonic ballet, which was imitated in Russia as well as other countries. His three ballets *Swan Lake, Sleeping Beauty,* and the *Nutcracker* were presented in Moscow between 1877 and 1892. In these fable-fantasies, Tchaikovsky included traditional dance motifs and folklore from various countries, all within a well-orchestrated symphonic framework.

Alexander Borodin
Modest Mussorgsky
Nikolay Rimsky-Korsakov

During the last half of the nineteenth century, three St. Petersburg, Russia, musicians, Alexander Borodin, Modest Mussorgsky, and Nikolay Rimsky-Korsakov, tried to resurrect Russia's musical heritage as well as found a Russian school of music. Borodin, a professor of chemistry, was dedicated to composing as well as to studying Russian songs. His colorful opera *Prince Igor* vividly portrays ancient Russian history and life.

Basing his compositions on traditional Russian music, especially the songs of its people, Mussorgsky, who died in 1881, created an independent musical style. A self-taught composer, his bold passages didn't fit the accepted rules, and today they sound extraordinarily modern. With the Imperial Theater Commission opposed to his strong revolutionary stand, Mussorgsky's operas *Boris Godunov* and *Khovanshchina* were never officially performed during his lifetime. Rimsky-Korsakov, a professor of composition at the St. Petersburg Conservatory, revised the operas for fear they would be censored so that it was some time before Mussorgsky's original operas became known.

As a professional musician, Rimsky-Korsakov, who was younger than the others, corrected, transcribed, and orchestrated their compositions to bring out their original spirit. He worked up until his death in 1908 to ensure that his friends' operas survived.

Patriotic Russian composers made Russia itself the leading character of their operas.

Bedřich Smetana

Although Bedřich Smetana served as a musician for two Austrian emperors, he never gave up hope that his Bohemian homeland would free itself from Austria. When his most celebrated opera, the comedy *The Bartered Bride*, which expressed the soul of the Bohemian people, had its one hundredth successful performance with Smetana in the audience, the composer was very sick and totally deaf. He died some time later in an asylum.

Smetana also composed many instrumental works, the best known being his symphonic poems collected under the title *My Country*, which described the Bohemian landscape and its people. *The Moldau* follows that river from its first drops at its source (expressed by notes played like drops of water) to its majestic meeting with the Danube, embodied by a full orchestra.

During his three years in America as director of the National Conservatory of Music in New York, Dvořák lived in this house.

Antonín Dvořák

A deeply religious family man, Antonín Dvořák made Czechoslovakian music known to the world. His *Slavonic Dances* for four-handed piano made him famous in 1878, and a few years later, when he presented his *Stabat Mater* in London, he was hailed as the new Handel. Appointed director of the New York Conservatory, Dvořák traveled throughout the United States, where he became interested in the music of blacks and American Indians. Echoes of American folklore, combined with Slavic motifs, can be heard in his famous symphony *From the New World*, composed during his stay in America. Dvořák's Concerto for Violoncello is another of his more frequently performed works.

Isaac Albéniz

Spain has always been unjustly treated as the land of castanets and tambourines. This image was perpetuated by foreign musicians who knew Spain only superficially and saw it as an exotic place, to be treated fancifully without regard to its true musical origins, and by Spanish musicians who found it expedient to export a readily acceptable music.

Because Spanish music had been so badly represented in Europe, during the nineteenth century Spanish musicians were determined to interpret the soul of their country by uncovering the ancient roots of their folk music and describing Spanish culture.

Isaac Albéniz finally did justice to the rich traditions of Spain with *Iberia* and *España,* compositions that elaborated folk-song motifs and transformed them into personal remembrances. He was always nostalgic for his native land, a feeling reflected in his music, but produced his best work while living in Paris.

Albéniz was a child prodigy. He was only four years old when he debuted as a pianist, in a Barcelona theater.

Enrique Granados

The music of Enrique Granados, especially his *Poetic Scenes* and *Romantic Scenes,* is often languid and melancholy. Among his masterpieces are the *Goyescas,* compositions inspired by the paintings of Francisco Goya. Granados fused Spanish popular tradition with the Romantic musical vocabulary common to all of Europe, but particularly in the twelve *Spanish Dances* and the *Goyescas,* his fresh rhythms and original melodies evoke the spirit of the land and people of Spain, without ever becoming simplistic or predictable.

Granados died in 1916, when a torpedo fired from a German submarine hit the ship on which he and his wife were traveling.

Along with Albéniz and Granados among the great Spanish composers of the late 1800s and early 1900s, we should also remember Manuel de Falla. He too is closely associated with his native land and evokes it in his own works, as in his first great composition, *Nights in the Gardens of Spain.* Spain and its popular music are brought to life in the lively rhythms of de Falla's ballets, among them *El amor brujo* (Love, the Magician) and *El sombrero de tres picos* (The Three-Cornered Hat).

In addition, de Falla created a masterful *Don Quixote* and *El retablo de maese Pedro* (The Puppet Theater of Master Pedro), in which a young boy takes the role of the theater showman.

Richard Strauss

Even if he lived until 1949, Richard Strauss, born in Munich in 1864, remained decidedly a personality tied to the nineteenth century. He was the last heir of Wagnerian late Romanticism and the great orchestrations of Berlioz and Liszt. Strauss excelled in many genres. He perfected the symphonic poem: descriptive "program" music based on the interpretation of the lives of famous people (*Don Quixote*), or of stories or events (*Ein Heldenleben*—A Hero's Life). He wrote many operas, including the world-famous *Rosenkavalier* (The Knight of the Rose), and his *Lieder* (songs) are perhaps his finest contributions to music. Strauss, in some of his works such as the opera *Elektra*, utilized difficult and elaborate musical forms, but later in life he returned to the traditional harmonies of classicism.

While many German musicians emigrated to America at the advent of Nazism, Strauss was made president of the Musikkammer of the Third Reich in 1933, for which he was severely criticized. He left the post in 1935 and after the war departed his country for Switzerland.

Richard Strauss was born into a family of musicians and was discovered as a young man by the great orchestral conductor Hans von Bülow.

Despite his success as a conductor, Mahler resigned in order to compose full-time.

Gustav Mahler

A Bohemian (Bohemia is now part of Czechoslovakia) and a Jew, Gustav Mahler had great difficulties in the German musical world of the late nineteenth and early twentieth centuries. The presence of the traditionalist Brahms on the jury of the Beethoven Prize, and Wagner's widow, the nationalist Cosima Wagner, on the artistic commission of the Viennese theaters, made it difficult for the young Mahler to establish himself. However, Mahler was eventually able to assert himself, first as orchestra conductor in Prague, then in Leipzig, Budapest, and Hamburg. Finally, in 1897, he was nominated director of the Vienna Court Opera.

Possessing a profound orchestral knowledge, the talented Mahler was conductor of several important orchestras, but because his symphonies, which expressed the restlessness of the times, seemed detached, complex, and indecisive, they were unpopular with high-society audiences, who didn't want their music to make them uncomfortable. Furthermore, Mahler had "undesirable" friends, among them Arnold Schönberg, another Jewish composer who scandalized audiences by dissolving traditional harmonies, and Sigmund Freud, a Jewish doctor dedicated to the then suspect study called psychoanalysis.

After an unhappy trip to the United States in 1907–8, Mahler returned to Vienna to compose full time. Although he completed nine symphonies, he died in 1911 before he could finish the tenth. No other musician since Beethoven had exceeded nine symphonies.

Claude Debussy

Pelléas et Mélisande, *on which Debussy worked for ten years, signaled the birth of modern opera. Presented in Paris in 1902, it caused a scandal. The kindest remark made by a critic was that it was "a deadly bore."*

Toward the end of the nineteenth century there was a new and innovative artistic climate in Paris. A group of composers tried to free European music of its sentimentality as well as its dangerously nationalistic elements. They wished to return to "pure" music of sounds and their interrelationships.

The composer who most closely adhered to these ideals was probably Claude Debussy, who was well aware that in his compositions he was breaking down the forms of traditional music. At one point he abandoned his brief, elegant, and rather cold compositions to create his masterpiece, the more conventional *La mer* (The Sea).

Although *Les images* and the *Préludes* evoke intense emotions, they never reveal Debussy's innermost soul, so that a listener's senses and intellect are more involved than his or her heart. Coldness and intellectualism were also personal characteristics of Debussy, who tended to be eccentric, nonconformist, arrogant, and somewhat of a dandy.

Grieg worked and lived in a small house in Troldhaugen, Norway.

Edvard Grieg

When Claude Debussy attended a concert in Paris given by the Norwegian composer Edvard Grieg, he defined it with arrogance as "provincial trifle," and yet the music of Grieg has also been defined as impressionististic, and perhaps Debussy was more impressed than he wanted to admit. It was not Edvard Grieg's intent to oppose traditional harmonies, but this in fact came about simply because he utilized the themes and rhythms of his Norwegian homeland. Grieg, who studied Scandinavian folklore, became a leading exponent of Scandinavian nationalism and conducted orchestras throughout Europe, making Scandinavian music known.

Grieg's compositions, such as *Lyric Pieces* and *Scenes from Life,* mirror the life of the Northland, while his famous *Peer Gynt* orchestral suites were based on a verse drama by the modern dramatist Henrik Ibsen.

Maurice Ravel

Maurice Ravel was a Basque who drew his musical inspiration from the Spanish character traits of vigor and restrained feeling. Ravel's famous *Rapsodie espagnole* and *Boléro* treat the Spanish motifs with force and precision. Ravel, who was himself energetic and passionate, had a sensitivity to the interaction between the different sections of the orchestra that has never been surpassed. Within a framework of traditional European music, he used the most inventive and modern forms.

Ravel was trained in Paris at the same time as Debussy and received the same influences from the French cultural world, yet his compositions that bring impressionism most to mind, such as *Jeux d'eau* (Water Games), were written before the *Préludes* of Debussy. With regard to their personalities, Ravel was vigorous and passionate, while Debussy was languid and intellectual.

Ravel, who died in 1937, was the last important voice of classical music. He enjoyed great popularity during his lifetime. After World War I, he was sought after by all the major capitals of the world, and he toured widely until the early 1930s when he became ill.

In 1908 Ravel wrote a little jewel of a work for two pianos, Ma Mère l'Oye *(Mother Goose); expanded and orchestrated, it became a famous ballet.*

Jean Sibelius

Jean Sibelius was a late-Romantic composer who wrote about the ancient sagas and traditions of his native Finland in symphonic poem form. After studying in Berlin and Vienna, Sibelius returned to Helsinki, where he was professor at the local conservatory from 1892 to 1910. After the Finnish government granted him a pension so that he could spend all his time composing, he retired to a country house, leaving only to conduct his symphonies on European tours. Already honored by Finland, in 1927 Sibelius stopped writing music altogether.

Sibelius's compositions masterfully couple Finnish sagas with an awareness and appreciation of nature that his music expresses in majestic terms.

Sibelius's Finlandia *is a symphonic poem that describes dramatic Finnish landscape.*

Igor Stravinsky

Igor Stravinsky, the Russian-born composer, went to St. Petersburg University to study law, but soon found his interest was music. In the early 1900s, Sergei Diaghilev, the director of the *Ballets-Russes* (Russian Ballet), who was based in Paris, asked Stravinsky to write some ballet music. Pleased with Stravinsky's work, Diaghilev requested music for a new ballet, taken from a Russian fable. The new work was called *The Firebird,* and was a smash hit. It was followed by another masterpiece, *Petrouchka,* then, two years later, by the *Rite of Spring,* which caused a riot at its Paris premiere.

During World War I, Stravinsky lived in Switzerland, where he worked on compositions that condensed, broke up, then rearranged motifs and rhythms taken from centuries-old music, from "light" music, and from jazz. Between the two world wars, Stravinsky returned to traditional musical forms in order to anchor his music firmly in the past so that he could better understand the present and anticipate the future.

Pablo Picasso paints a portrait of Igor Stravinsky in 1920. The two artists, both of whom left a deep imprint on this century, were often compared because of the similarity of their creative directions.

Benjamin Britten

In his tragic opera of the sea, *Peter Grimes,*
performed for the first time in London in
1945, the Englishman Benjamin Britten
showed that he could use the advanced techniques of Debussy, Stravinsky, and
Schönberg, yet still reach a wide audience
with his music. Britten, who composed almost until his death, wrote in almost every
form, including operas, orchestral works,
choral works, solo works for the voice, and·
chamber music. His operas *The Turn of the
Screw* and *Death in Venice,* taken from a
book by Thomas Mann, are well known.
Many people consider him to be England's
greatest composer.

*Britten founded a small opera company that took
his work to many cities and countries.*

Louis Armstrong

New Orleans, at the mouth of the Mississippi, which became the melting pot of black musical experience, was the home of the blues—music that is rich with sensual passion and deep melancholy. Jazz, an unwritten music, is interpreted by the player, who becomes, therefore, the composer. Tradition has it that the musician improvises as he likes and then returns to harmonize with those with whom he is playing, either a small group or a very large group made up of wind instruments, trumpet, clarinet, saxophone, and double bass, as well as the guitar and banjo.

The King of Jazz is said to be the trumpet, but there is general agreement that Louis "Satchmo" Armstrong—trumpeter, singer, and band leader—was the King of Trumpets, a master of communication and spontaneity.

Louis Armstrong played on the Mississippi river-boats that operated out of New Orleans, his hometown and the cradle of jazz.

"Satchmo" was just as famous as a singer. A frequent show guest, he often sang with Ella Fitzgerald. Among his many tours throughout the world, those to Africa in 1956 and 1960 are particularly significant.

Benny Goodman

The 1930s in America was known as the Jazz Age, jazz having moved from blues to swing, with a new, exciting rhythm. Benny Goodman, an extraordinary clarinettist and an important figure in jazz, made his first record at seventeen, hitting the big time in 1936, when he formed his own big band. In 1938 he broke tradition at New York's elegant Carnegie Hall by playing jazz.

From then on, jazz was no longer just the music of black people, but of all America. In 1956 and 1972, the State Department sent Benny Goodman and his orchestra on a tour to present American music to the world.

Benny Goodman and his big band cut many records, played in films, and went on world tours.

Duke Ellington

Edward "Duke" Ellington was the top jazz personality on the East Coast. Although he was an excellent pianist and composer, perhaps his greatest talent lay in surrounding himself with the best musicians and soloists. As a band leader, Ellington struck just the right balance between the orchestra and the improvisation of the individual soloist, which enabled him to develop such orchestral suites as his *Black, Brown, and Beige Suite* of 1943. Onstage Duke knew how to ham it up and draw an audience into his spell.

Duke Ellington knew how to use to advantage the often exceptional jazz soloists in his band, giving them space in a performance. Nearly all his players stayed with him for good.

Paul McCartney   *Ringo Starr*   *John Lennon*   *George Harrison*

The Beatles

In the past thirty years popular, or pop, music has become ninety percent of all the music that is listened to, or at least, heard, in America and Europe. The success of pop music is due to the merging of various national traditions into one great current, rock, which has a clear and danceable rhythm, simple and easily remembered melodies, pleasing harmonic chords, and relatively few instrumental tone-colors.

Some of the innovative groups representing this commercial music, the Beatles in particular, have been myths since the 1960s, with their songs ever-popular. Who has never heard or sung "Yesterday" or "A Hard Day's Night"? And who has never heard of Paul McCartney, Ringo Starr, John Lennon, and George Harrison, the famed Beatles?

The Rolling Stones, another English group, sing more biting songs that are full of protest. Elvis Presley, the King of Rock and Roll, has millions of fans throughout the world despite his premature death, while the two voices and two guitars that probably best expressed the ideals of young people in the 1960s are those of Bob Dylan and Joan Baez, who still perform throughout the world.

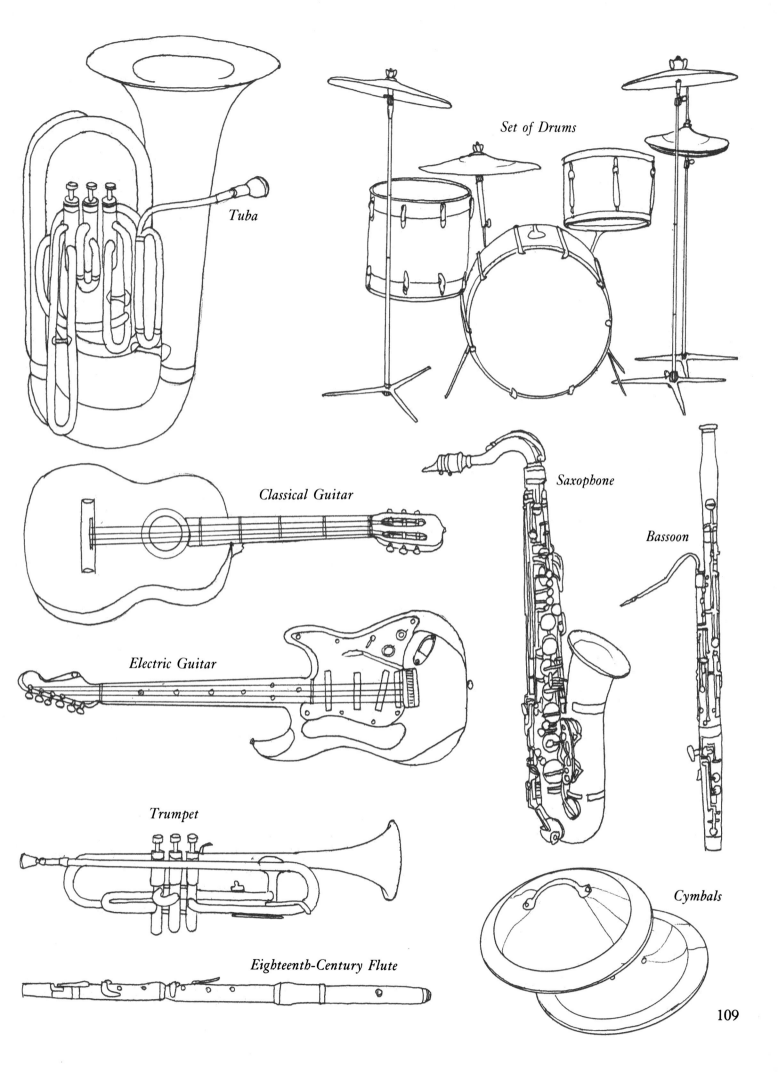

Tuba

Set of Drums

Classical Guitar

Saxophone

Bassoon

Electric Guitar

Trumpet

Cymbals

Eighteenth-Century Flute

109

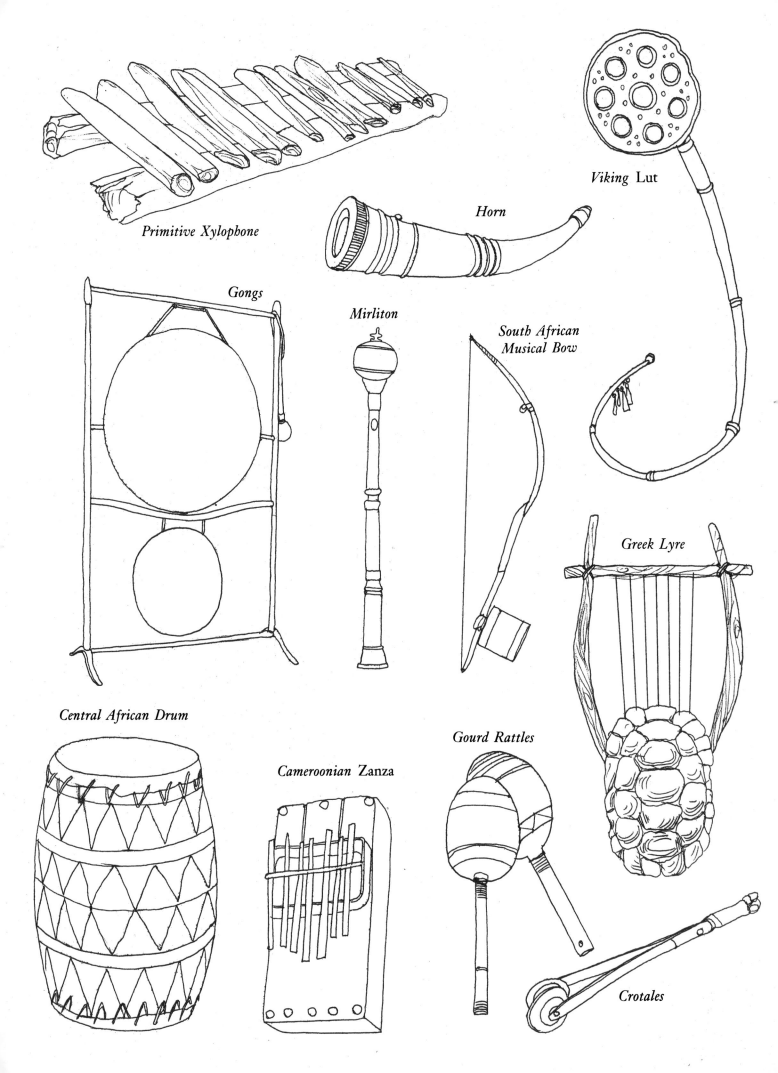

Primitive Xylophone

Horn

Viking Lut

Gongs

Mirliton

South African
Musical Bow

Greek Lyre

Central African Drum

Gourd Rattles

Cameroonian Zanza

Crotales

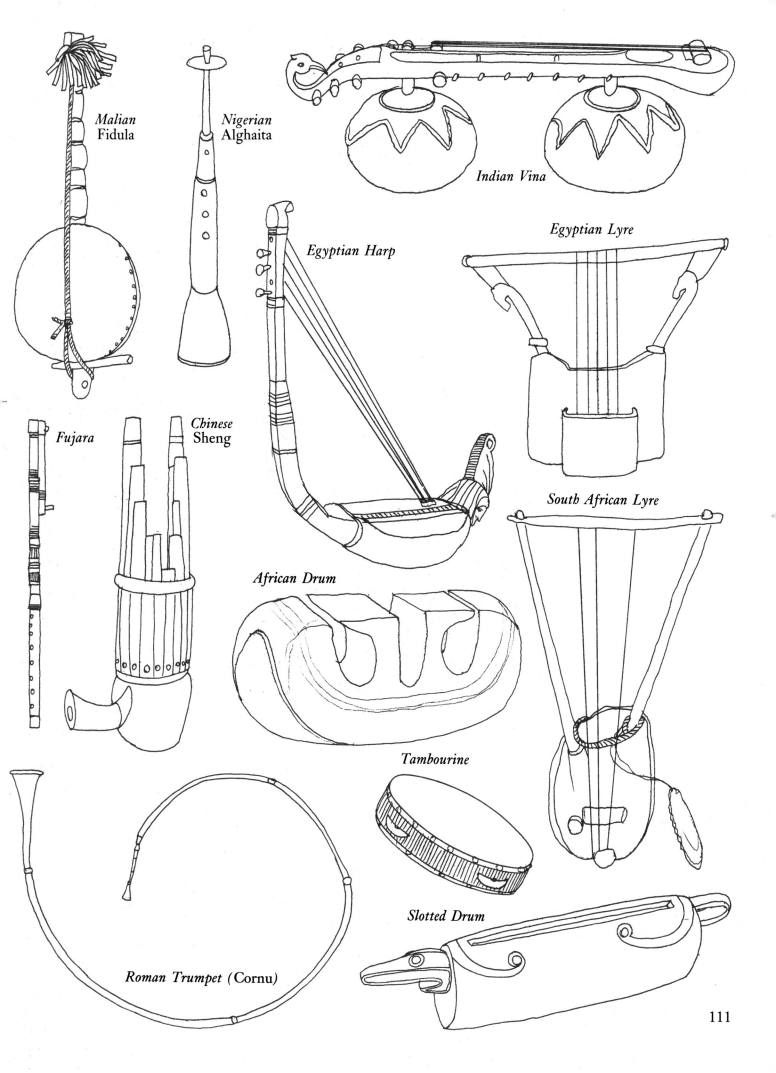

Malian Fidula

Nigerian Alghaita

Indian Vina

Egyptian Harp

Egyptian Lyre

Fujara

Chinese Sheng

South African Lyre

African Drum

Tambourine

Slotted Drum

Roman Trumpet (Cornu)

111

THE LIVES OF THE GREAT COMPOSERS

These brief biographies are intended to supplement the profiles of the composers with additional information. They are presented in chronological order.

GREGORY THE GREAT (Rome c.540–604) Pope Gregory was born into a wealthy family from which one member had already become pope. After withdrawing to a monastery, Gregory had seven new monasteries built with his own money in Italy, including the abbey of Sant' Andrea, which had been his family home. When Pope Pelagius II, who had taken Gregory out of his monastery and made him ambassador to Constantinople (now Istanbul, Turkey) died, Gregory was the unanimous choice for pope. He tried to avoid the nomination by sending a petition to the Greek emperor of Constantinople, but Roman authorities intercepted it and he was crowned as Gregory I on September 3, 590.

Pope Gregory, who is considered one of the four great "Doctors" of the Catholic Church, was declared a saint for his theological and moral works. He is also remembered for his liturgical reform and the *Antifonario*, a collection of all the songs in the official liturgy. According to tradition, he composed or rearranged many of them. He also ordered that the book which is the basis of the Church's sacred music be tied to St. Peter's altar with a golden chain.

ODO DE CLUGNY (c.879–Tours 942) Odo de Clugny, a Benedictine monk, was first a chorister in St. Martin's Church at Tours and then abbot of the monastery at Clugny. He was a music theorist and is responsible for naming the intervals between the notes and the substitution of Greek letters for the Latin ones. With the letter "A" he indicated the note "la" and then followed with "B, C, D, E, F, G" for the other notes of the first octave.

GUIDO D'AREZZO (Arezzo c.992–1050) Guido d'Arezzo, also known as Guido the Monk, was a Benedictine monk and teacher of music in the Cathedral of Arezzo. While at the abbey at Pomposa, he studied musical notation. He introduced the music staff of four lines and invented names for the tones of the notes which corresponded to the first syllable of the verses of a well-known hymn, with each note toned a pitch higher than the one before it. The names Guido gave the notes are still used in Italy and France. A great musician and teacher, Guido retired in 1029 to a monastery.

GUILLAUME DE MACHAUT (Rheims c.1300–1377) As a young man, Guillaume de Machaut was a poet, an adventurer, and musician at the court of King John of Bohemia. After the king's death, he was secretary to the king's daughter, later Queen of France. During the Hundred Years War between France and England,

Guillaume helped defend the French city of Rheims. His love for a young girl inspired him in 1365 to write a tale that alternated with songs, followed by *La prise d'Alexandrie* (The Capture of Alexandria [Egypt]), a poem about the Crusades. Because he organized all his writings and musical compositions for publication in his old age, many have survived. Guillaume's *Mass of Notre-Dame* is the first polyphonic mass written entirely by one author.

KONRAD PAUMANN (Nuremberg c.1415–Munich 1473) Blind from birth, Paumann, who became an organ virtuoso and is considered the father of German organ tradition, composed important collections of exercises or preludes called *Fundamentum organisandi*. He was also a virtuoso on the harp, the lute, and the flute.

JOSQUIN DESPRÈS (Beaurevoir c.1440–Condé-sur-l'Escaut, c.1521). When French-Flemish composer Desprès was about twenty, he was a chorister, first in Milan and then in the chapel of Duke Galeazzo Maria Sforza, in Milan, Italy, and from 1486 to 1494, in the papal choir in Rome. From there he went to the court of the powerful Este family at Ferrara, Italy, and in 1501 was in Paris at the chapel of King Louis XII. In his final years he was canon of the Cathedral chapter of Condé. Josquin wrote over twenty masses, about ninety motets, and more than thirty secular compositions for both voices and instruments. During the sixteenth and seventeenth centuries, Josquin's works, which were both handwritten and printed, were widely distributed in Europe.

ANDREA GABRIELI (Venice c.1510–1586) Andrea Gabrieli was probably an organist at the Cathedral of Verona, Italy, about 1550. From 1564 until his death, he was organist at St. Mark's Cathedral in Venice. Famous as an organist, he was even better known as a teacher, drawing students from all over Europe. His vocal compositions, both secular and religious, included 110 motets for four to twelve voices, four masses (with a *Gloria* for sixteen voices), and nearly 250 madrigals for three to twelve voices as well as concertos for every type of instrument. Gabrieli's famous *L'Edippo tiranno* (Oedipus the Tyrant), a choral commentary on Sophocles' tragedy, was performed at the opening of the Olympic Theater in Vicenza, Italy, in 1585.

GIOVANNI PIERLUIGI DE PALESTRINA (Palestrina 1525–Rome 1594) As a boy, Giovanni was a chorister at the Palestrina Cathedral. When the Bishop of Palestrina was elected pope (Julius III), he nominated Giovanni choirmaster, first of the Julian Chapel and then of the Sistine Chapel. After Giovanni was dismissed by the Vatican because he was married, he became choir director of St. John Lateran and then choir director of Santa Maria Maggiore. At the same time, he composed secular music, organizing performances in the famous Villa d'Este at Tivoli, near Rome.

After his first wife died, Giovanni married a wealthy woman and from then on had the money to dedicate himself entirely to composing and publishing. Although he wrote nearly one hundred madrigals, most of his compositions were sacred music, with more than one hundred masses and about two hundred and fifty motets including the *Mass for Pope Marcellus II*, an example of the simplicity that the Council of Trent in its reforms imposed on sacred music.

ORLANDO DI LASSO (Mons c.1532–Munich 1594) Orlando di Lasso was a Flemish composer who distinguished himself as a choirboy in the Church of St. Nicholas in Mons. From 1544 he worked for Ferdinando Gonzaga, Viceroy of Sicily, until 1549, when he went into the service of a Neapolitan nobleman. From 1553 to 1554 he was choirmaster at St. John Lateran in Rome, where he met Pierluigi da Palestrina.

Returning for some years to Flanders, Orlando published his first collection of sacred motets and secular madrigals. In 1556 he went into the service of Albert V, Duke of Bavaria, as tenor and then as choirmaster, at which time he composed the seven *Penitential Psalms*. Famous throughout Europe, Orlando published his *Book of Madrigals* in Venice in 1556. Sought after by various royal courts, he preferred to live in Munich, where he died in 1594, leaving behind fifty-eight masses for four and eight voices, 546 motets for two to twelve voices, 101 *Magnificat*s, and many other compositions, including 187 madrigals, ninety-three German *Lieder*, and 146 French *Chansons*.

JOHN DOWLAND (Dublin 1562–London 1626) John Dowland was a great lutanist and composer of airs and songs, who entered the service of the English ambassador in Paris before he was twenty. After receiving his Bachelor of Music at Oxford and Cambridge, he traveled throughout Europe, remaining for some time in Italy.

After serving as lutanist at the Danish court from 1598 to 1612, Dowland became musician at the English court where he wrote several collections of songs, some in the popular style and some of which were influenced by the Italian madrigal. In 1604 he wrote the melancholy compositions for lute and viola called *Lachrymae* (Tears), for which he was known as "Doleful Dowland."

CLAUDIO MONTEVERDI (Cremona 1567–Venice 1643) At the age of twenty, Monteverdi was already well known in Europe for his first six books of madrigals. While serving as viola player and chorister and then as music-master at the Duke of Mantua's court, Monteverdi traveled extensively throughout Europe. He also contributed major masterpieces to opera. *Orfeo*, written in 1607, was considered to be the first opera in history and the foundation of operas to come.

When his patron, Duke Vincent Gonzago, died, Monteverdi moved to Venice to serve as choirmaster of the Venetian Republic. After the death of his wife, he became a priest and wrote many sacred compositions with the same passionate spirit that marked all of his work.

JEAN-BAPTISTE LULLY (Florence 1632–Paris 1687) Although Lully was born in Italy, because of his talent as a violinist and dancer, at the age of thirteen he was taken to France where he spent the rest of his life at the court of King Louis XIV. In collaboration with the dramatist Corneille, Lully wrote thirteen comedy-ballets which signaled the beginning of French opera. With the poet Philippe Quinault, Lully also composed a series of "lyric tragedies" that competed with the Italian opera that had been introduced earlier in France by Cardinal Mazarin.

HENRY PURCELL (London c.1659–1695) Henry Purcell, who began his career as a chorister in the English Chapel Royal, was nominated composer for the court orchestra in 1677, becoming organist in 1679 at Westminster Abbey, where he was later buried. Purcell also served in the court of James II and William III. When the king returned to London, Purcell wrote the *Welcome Songs,* six odes for Queen Mary's birthday, and hymns for court occasions such as the coronation of James II.

Although Purcell's fame is mainly based on music for the theater, to which he devoted the last years of his short life, he also composed instrumental music, songs, mostly for three voices, and an opera, *Dido and Aeneas.*

ALESSANDRO SCARLATTI (Palermo 1660–Naples 1725) Scarlatti married at an early age and had ten children, of whom the sixth, Domenico, also became famous. Although Scarlatti tried to transfer with Domenico to Florence from Naples where he had served as choirmaster since 1684, his efforts failed and father and son had to remain in Naples.

Scarlatti was the greatest representative of the so-called "Neapolitan school" of opera to which he contributed sixty-five works as well as rewriting other composers' works. As a representative of the "Italian" flavor, he influenced the European musicians of his time, including Bach and Handel.

ANTONIO VIVALDI (Venice 1678–Vienna 1741) Antonio Vivaldi, whose violinist-father taught him to play the violin, became an ordained priest and a teacher at Venice's Ospedale della Pietà, an institution for female orphans and abandoned girls. Vivaldi wrote the major part of his cantatas and concertos for the girls, to be performed every Sunday. His sacred music was also played in St. Mark's Cathedral, a huge, many-domed building with extraordinary acoustics.

Vivaldi's musical output was enormous, but because it was discovered only a few decades ago, it is not yet all catalogued. So far, 450 concertos and forty-six operas have been found, in addition to symphonies, sonatas, and sacred compositions. Vivaldi's two main collections of concertos are *L'estro armonico* and *Il cimento dell'armonia e dell'invenzione*. His most famous opera is *Orlando furioso*. The two *Dixit*, *The Four Seasons*, and the two *Magnificats* are also famous. This great musician died in Vienna in 1741 in poverty.

JEAN-PHILIPPE RAMEAU (Dijon 1683–Paris 1764) In his youth Rameau dedicated himself to the harpsichord, publishing three books of compositions. His theoretical studies of harmony have earned him fame as one of the principal codifiers of the rules of musical composition and he is said to be the creator of modern harmony. Nevertheless, he is known primarily for his splendid operas and opera-ballets and his novel theories, which resulted in a quarrel between his supporters and those who favored the more traditional music of Lully. The same types of attacks that were made against Wagner a century later were made against Rameau: absence of melody and the emphasis on "discords" and noise. Rameau's new style was admired by the thinkers of the French Enlightenment—the forerunners of the French Revolution of 1789.

JOHANN SEBASTIAN BACH (Eisenach 1685–Leipzig 1750) Son of a violinist, Johann Sebastian Bach was introduced to music by his father and older brother. After a brief period as violinist in the ducal orchestra of Weimar, Bach became organist at the church at Arnstadt, where he was criticized for elaborating too much on the accompaniment of the chorale. He consequently transferred, first to Mühlhausen and then to Weimar, where he composed the six *Brandenburg Concertos*. In 1723 Bach became cantor at the Thomasschule in Leipzig, his home for life, where he conducted his *Passion According to St. John* in 1724 and the *Passion According to St. Matthew* in 1729.

Because of Bach's fame as an organ virtuoso, organ builders frequently consulted him. It was only much later that he was recognized as a composer. Bach wrote both for local occasions and for himself. He probably wrote the eight Concertos for Harpsichord for his ten children, who were all accomplished musicians. In 1734 he wrote the Italian Concerto for the harpsichord, in which he transposed the style used by Italian musicians for other instruments, also composing for the harpsichord the six *English Suites* in the same manner and the six *French Suites*, as well as the *Goldberg Variations*. The art of the harpsichord reached its peak in Bach's two books, *The Well-Tempered Clavier*, each of which contained twenty-four compositions.

Bach, who also wrote sonatas for violin, violoncello, flute, and lute, composed many works for the organ, which include entire collections of chorales and sonatas. Although he was nearly blind, Bach dedicated the last years of his life to composing his monumental work *The Art of the Fugue*.

DOMENICO SCARLATTI (Naples 1685–Madrid 1757) Domenico Scarlatti was the sixth son of Alessandro Scarlatti, from whom he received his musical training. He later studied in Venice, where he knew Vivaldi and Handel. Although he made his public debut with opera, from the time he went to the Portuguese court in Lisbon in 1720, he dedicated himself primarily to sacred music. After moving to the court of Madrid, he not only became the "teacher of the Catholic Kings," but was also surrounded by talented students such as Antonio Soler. The historical importance of Domenico Scarlatti rests on his compositions for the harpsichord, although none were published during his lifetime.

GEORG FRIDERIC HANDEL (Halle 1685–London 1759) Although Handel began composing music when he was ten, his father, a barber-surgeon, enrolled him in law school. After a year Handel left to earn his living playing in an orchestra in Hamburg, Germany, where he presented his first opera, *Almira*, in 1705. He lived in Italy for some years, where the best of the Italian musicians admired his operas and oratorios.

In 1711 he went to London, where he settled permanently, becoming a British subject in 1726. For thirty-five years Handel was central to English musical life, and his operas were usually moneymakers. Handel's fame today, however, rests on his oratorios, the first of which, *Esther* (1732), was a great success, with his *Messiah* experiencing its first triumphant performance in Dublin in 1742. While working on the oratorio *Jephtha*, Handel underwent eye surgery, subsequently losing his sight. Nonetheless, he continued to conduct until his death.

Handel composed twenty-two oratorios and forty operas, as well as compositions for sacred and instrumental chamber music.

BENEDETTO MARCELLO (Venice 1686–Brescia 1739) Benedetto Marcello, who came from a noble Venetian family, worked for the Venetian government at Pola for many years, after which he became a court official at Brescia. A cultured man with many interests, Marcello dedicated himself to both literature and music, leaving behind concertos, sonatas, and songs. He is famous for his comedy *Il teatro alla moda* (The Stylish Theater), in which he satirizes opera and the temperamental prima donnas of his day.

BALDASSARRE GALUPPI (Venice 1706–1785) Called "il Buranello" because he was born on the Venetian island of Burano, Baldassarre Galuppi, a prolific composer, was music-master of St. Mark's Cathedral. *L'Arcadia in Brenta* (A Paradise in Brenta), *Il paese di cuccagna* (The Land of Milk and Honey), and *Il filosofo di campagna* (The Country Philosopher), written in collaboration with the playwright Goldoni, were among the first comic operas. Galuppi also wrote eighty-five sonatas for the harpsichord.

GIOVANNI BATTISTA PERGOLESI (Jesi 1710–Pozzuoli 1736) Giovanni Battista Pergolesi, the son of a land surveyor, was helped in his musical career by a local nobleman. He also studied at the Conservatorio dei Poveri di Gesu Cristo in Naples, where he developed his extraordinary talent. His *Stabat Mater* for soprano, contralto, and orchestra, a devotional work dedicated to the Virgin Mary, written shortly before his death at twenty-six of tuberculosis, is a masterpiece. His comic operas, such as *Lo frate 'nammorato* (The Monk in Love) and *La serva padrona* (The Maid as Mistress), composed in the typical Neapolitan style, became enormously successful in Europe.

CHRISTOPH WILLIBALD GLUCK (Frasbach 1714–Vienna 1787) Although Gluck was not encouraged musically by his family, under the guidance of Giovanni Sammartini, he made his debut as an opera composer in Milan. After a trip to London, during which he met Handel, Gluck settled in Vienna, where he collaborated with the librettist Ranieri de Calzabigi in the successful attempt to reform opera—to free it from dependence on temperamental singers. Although he had already composed over thirty traditional operas, when he took his "reform" operas to Paris, a controversy was started between his supporters and those of Niccolò Piccinni, who continued to compose opera "all'italiana," rejecting his theories.

His last opera, *Echo and Narcissus,* was a failure, and Gluck returned to Vienna and stopped composing. Although his ideas about serious opera were not immediately followed, other composers later adopted them. Gluck's works are still performed, the most famous of which is *Orpheus and Eurydice.*

NICCOLÒ PICCINNI (Bari 1728–Paris 1800) Niccolò Piccinni had his first success as an opera composer in Naples, where he had studied at the Conservatorio Sant'Onofrio. In 1760 he presented in Rome *Cecchina ossia la buona figliola* (Cecchina, or, The Obedient Daughter), based on Carlo Goldoni's libretto, which gained him immediate fame in Europe. Although he was invited to Paris in 1776 to cash in on the French taste for Italian opera, as opposed to Gluck's "reform" operas, Piccinni used some of Gluck's innovations, especially in his opera *Didone* (Dido).

Because he had been in Paris during the French Revolution, when Piccinni returned to Naples, he was put under house arrest for four years on the suspicion of having revolutionary ideas. Although he wrote about 120 operas, the success of the next generation of Italian opera composers caused him to be nearly forgotten.

FRANZ JOSEPH HAYDN (Rohrau 1732–Vienna 1809) Franz Joseph Haydn was a farmer's son. He was a boy soprano in the St. Stephen's Cathedral choir in Vienna at the age of eight, earned his living playing in an orchestra and accompanying singers and violinists on the harpsichord when his voice changed. In 1761 he entered the service of the princes Esterházy, who had a theater with a permanent orchestra and singers in their Hungarian castle. Considered a member of the family, Haydn spent thirty years there, while the publications of his compositions brought him fame throughout Europe. The young Mozart admired and was influenced by Haydn, while Beethoven was Haydn's student for a short time. When Prince Nikolaus Esterházy died, Haydn was dismissed by his son with a pension for life, whereupon he visited London from 1790 to 1792 and from 1794 to 1795, with Oxford University conferring a doctorate on him.

Of Haydn's 108 symphonies, most were for the Esterházy orchestra, while the *London* and the *Paris* were written for the Paris Opera orchestra. Out of eighty-three quartets, Haydn's first quartets for two violins, viola, and violoncello were commissioned by a Viennese gentleman. His six *Russian Quartets* were dedicated to the Grand Duke Pavel Petrovic, and his six *Prussian Quartets* were dedicated to King Frederick William II of Prussia. Haydn also composed oratorios, numerous concertos for different instruments, and sonatas for the piano as well as collaborating with the librettist Goldoni on theatrical works.

GIOVANNI PAISIELLO (Taranto 1740–Naples 1816) Paisiello, who studied at the Conservatorio Sant'Onofrio in Naples, had his first opera successes in Bologna, gaining fame in both serious and comic opera in Naples. At the height of his success, he went to St. Petersburg, where the Empress Catherine the Great of Russia appointed him choirmaster and superintendent of the Italian Opera. Among other works, in 1782 he composed the opera called *The Barber of Seville,* based on the French play *The Marriage of Figaro.* (Mozart and Rossini later also used this play for their operas.)

Paisiello, who found himself caught up in Russian court-theater intrigue and even arrested, returned to Naples. In 1789, at the royal palace of Caserta, he presented his opera *Nina pazza per amore* (Nina Mad for Love), which is still performed today. In 1803 he went to Paris to write operas for Napoleon, but after Napoleon's fall, Paisiello was shunted aside. He wrote over one hundred operas as well as other works.

LUIGI BOCCHERINI (Lucca 1743–Madrid 1805) Luigi Boccherini, who came from a family of musicians and ballet dancers, received his first musical education from his father, which he completed in Rome. At eighteen he began his career as a violoncellist, also composing so much for all musical forms—trios, quartets, quintets, sonatas, etc.—that the job of cataloguing and dating all his works continues to this day to be an almost insurmountable task.

When Boccherini was twenty-five, he became the musician of don Luis, brother of King Charles III of Spain. After the death of both brothers, his new patron was Frederick William II of Prussia, who gave Boccherini a salary in return for writing new compositions. These came to a total of forty quintets, thirty quartets, and ten trios. When Napoleon invaded Prussia, Boccherini became musician to Napoleon's brother Lucien Bonaparte but after Napoleon's defeat, Boccherini's new patron became the King of Spain, who paid him badly. Boccherini is admired for his melodiousness, not for his originality.

DOMENICO CIMAROSA (Aversa 1749–Venice 1801) Although Domenico Cimarosa, an orphan, studied music in Loreto, he began his musical career in Naples. His first success was his comic opera Giannina e Bernardone (Joan and Bernard), performed in Venice in 1781. Following in Paisiello's footsteps, Cimarosa worked at the court of St. Petersburg, Russia, for five years, but with only modest recognition. He returned to Italy in 1791.

After working in Vienna, Cimarosa was commissioned to write his opera Il matrimonio segreto (The Secret Marriage), after which he returned to Naples in 1794 where his Le astuzie femminili (Women's Wiles) was also a success. The immensely popular Cimarosa was imprisoned in 1799 for revolutionary activities, and he may have been poisoned by the Queen of Naples. In addition to some seventy operas, Cimarosa also composed instrumental music, leaving dozens of sonatas for harpsichord and piano. His forte was comic opera, some of which are still performed.

WOLFGANG AMADEUS MOZART (Salzburg 1756–Vienna 1791) Wolfgang Amadeus Mozart's father, Leopold, who was Archbishop of Salzburg, concertmaster as well as a composer, was intensely concerned with the musical education of his children. When his sister Nannerl Mozart was ten and Wolfgang was six, they gave their first concert at the court of Munich, Bavaria, followed immediately by a concert for Empress Maria Theresa of Austria. Wolfgang triumphed, and his father took him on tour through Germany and then on to Paris and London. At eleven, Wolfgang composed his first comic opera, La finta semplice (The False Simpleton), which was produced when he was twelve. Despite Wolfgang's poor health, his father took him to Italy in 1769, where

he gave concerts and met prominent Italian musicians. After the Archbishop of Salzburg's death in 1772, the new archbishop proved to be hostile to the Mozart family. Forced to leave Salzburg, Wolfgang went to Paris with his mother, who died there in 1778.

The success of his 1781 opera Idomeneo re di Creta (Idomeneo, King of Crete) in Munich, convinced Mozart to try his fortune in Vienna. Commissioned by the Austrian Emperor Joseph II to put on an opera at the court theater, Mozart wrote Die Entführung aus dem Serail (The Rescue from the Harem), a comedy which is considered the beginning of German opera. Three masterpieces came out of his meeting with the Venetian poet Lorenzo da Ponte, Le nozze di Figaro (The Marriage of Figaro), Don Giovanni, and Così fan tutte (Women Are Like That).

Joseph II named Mozart "chamber musician" at a modest salary but Mozart, who was alone, poor, and in failing health in Vienna, with his father dead and his relationship with his wife unhappy, was obsessed by thoughts of death. A stranger commissioned a Requiem Mass, paying Mozart a handsome advance before disappearing. Mozart wrote Der Zauberflöte (The Magic Flute) for a small Viennese theater, then, feeling himself near death, he began his Requiem but died on December 5, 1791, without finishing it.

Mozart wrote immense amounts of exquisite music in every known form. No one has ever succeeded in summarizing the achievements of this incredible genius who during his lifetime received only a fraction of the recognition due him.

LUDWIG VAN BEETHOVEN (Bonn 1770–Vienna 1827) Although his father was a Flemish chorister in Bonn, young Ludwig's contact with the intellectual life of the day was through the Breuning family, to whom he gave piano lessons. The Archbishop of Bonn, who hired Beethoven as organist in 1784, also had him study under Haydn in Vienna, where Beethoven gave his first public concert in 1795, earning him great praise.

Beethoven's years of greatest productivity were between 1795 and 1815, when he composed 8 of his 9 symphonies; 27 of his 32 sonatas for violin and piano and for violoncello and piano; 11 of his 16 quartets; his only opera, Fidelio; the Lieder; and masses. At the time of his last public concert for the Vienna Congress in 1815, Beethoven was already quite deaf. When he became totally deaf, his isolation became total. Out of it came his last masterpiece, five sonatas for piano, five quartets for harp, the Missa Solemnis, and the Ninth Symphony. Beethoven's artistic achievements, so different from those of Mozart, are so vast that they defy description. When the "van" was added to his name, he became a member of the aristocracy, who treated him as an equal—something unheard of at the time. Beethoven began as a classical composer, but by the end of his life his late works had become so advanced that they were considered unplayable for fifty years.

NICCOLÒ PAGANINI (Genoa 1782–Nice 1840) Niccolò Paganini, born into poverty, was an accomplished violinist by the age of thirteen. He began an amazing career as a concert artist after studying two years at the school of Parma, Italy. After triumphing in all the major Italian cities, Paganini toured Vienna, Prague, Warsaw, Berlin, and, in 1831, Paris and London. Paganini was a passionate man—a gambler and lover of many women who also managed to earn a fortune, which he shared generously. Paganini's works include twenty-four *Capricci* for Solo Violin, six Concertos for Violin and Orchestra, and the Sonatas for One String. An excellent guitarist, he also left twelve Sonatas for Violin and Guitar and twenty-four Quartets for Violin, Guitar, Viola, and Violoncello.

CARL MARIA VON WEBER (Eutin 1786–London 1826) Weber's father was musical director of a traveling theatrical company so Carl received a good background in music, came to know the music of his country, and met influential people. Later Weber traveled to different cities as orchestral director. While he was director of the opera theaters in Prague, Bohemia, and Dresden, Germany, he worked on plans for a German national theater that would express the new Romantic ideas in contrast to traditional Italian opera. Weber's 1820 opera *Der Freischütz* was the first German Romantic opera. His last opera, perhaps his best, *Oberon*, taken from Shakespeare's *A Midsummer Night's Dream*, was presented at Covent Garden, London, in 1826.

GIOACCHINO ROSSINI (Pesaro 1792–Paris 1868) His father was a trumpet player and his mother was an opera singer. He began composing as a child. By the time he had entered the local high school at Bologna, he had already written an opera. When he finished his studies, he made his debut in Venice in 1810 with the comic opera *La cambiale di matrimonio* (The Marriage Promise). At the age of twenty Rossini wrote his first serious opera, *Tancredi*, and the comic opera *L'Italiana in Algeri* (The Italian Girl in Algeria). At first, he primarily wrote comic operas. Then, while a theater director in Naples from 1815 to 1822, he composed mainly serious operas: *Otello, Maometto* (Mohammed), *La donna del lago* (The Lady of the Lake), and many others.

In 1823 Rossini left the Italian theater and went first to Vienna, then to London, finally settling in Paris, where he adapted some of his operas to the current French taste, while also composing for the Paris Opéra. His last Parisian opera was the immensely successful *Guillaume Tell* (William Tell, 1829), after which he lived "in silence," the result of nervous exhaustion, although during periods of improved health he did continue to compose. *Giovanna d'Arco* (Joan of Arc) and the *Stabat Mater* are from that period, while in 1863 he wrote his last work, the *Petite messe solennelle*—a "solemn Mass."

FRANZ SCHUBERT (Vienna 1797–1828) Although young Franz Schubert was studying composition under Antonio Salieri, Mozart's rival, he briefly followed in his schoolmaster-father's footsteps. But his talents were evident, and before he was twenty had composed the incredible number of five hundred *Lieder*, a type of music he found particularly congenial because these delicate songs expressed his emotional side as well as being short. When Schubert was hired as music-master for the young Esterházy princesses, he left schoolteaching forever and began a period of immense creativity, composing among other works the "Trout" quintet, the *Wanderer Fantasy* and the *Unfinished Symphony*. (His complete works fill forty volumes.)

In 1822 Schubert nearly died, and although very sick, he resumed composing, contributing another hundred or more *Lieder* as well as orchestral, piano, and chamber works. He died very young, and was buried next to Beethoven. All of Schubert's works are prized for their melodiousness and delicacy. His life was a continual struggle for survival, yet he was sociable and loved by his many friends. All of his music except his operas is played today.

GAETANO DONIZETTI (Bergamo 1797–1848) Gaetano Donizetti, who came from a poor family, attended Bergamo's music school where he was discovered by Simone Mayr, a German musician who became Donizetti's instructor until 1815 when he sent Donizetti to the music high school in Bologna. Although he first wrote mediocre lyric operas, Donizetti produced *Anna Bolena* in 1830 to general acclaim in Milan. Moving to Naples as director of composition and director of the Regi Theater, Donizetti presented a series of operas which included *Lucia di Lammermoor*. With the help of Rossini, Donizetti made his debut in Paris in 1838 with *La figlia del reggimento* (The Daughter of the Regiment), followed by other successes such as *Don Pasquale*. While in Paris, Donizetti suffered a stroke, returning to Bergamo where he died three years later.

VINCENZO BELLINI (Catania 1801–Paris 1835) Born into a family of musicians, Vincenzo Bellini, who composed sacred and secular songs for churches and for private performances at an early age, completed his studies in Naples with money from the town council. Although the final exam there gained him entrance to San Carlo, in order to forget his love for an aristocratic young woman, he transferred to Milan where he presented his opera *Il pirata* (The Pirate) at La Scala in 1827. Gaining success with *I Capuleti e i Montecchi* (The Capulets and the Montagues), *La sonnambula* (The Sleepwalker), and *Norma*, Bellini was sought after by Milan's best salons. Bellini produced *I Puritani* (The Puritans) in 1833 for the Italian theater in Paris, dying tragically only a short time later.

HECTOR BERLIOZ (Isère 1808–Paris 1869) After studying music in his home city, Hector Berlioz went to Paris at eighteen where he won the Grand Prix de Rome which, in turn, took him to Rome for a year. Returning to Paris, he fell in love with the English actress Harriet Smithson, consequently writing his best-known work, the *Symphonie fantastique*. Although Berlioz was admired by Liszt, Wagner, and Paganini, he had less success with the public, and his opera *Benvenuto Cellini* failed in 1838. Berlioz's other grand opera, *Les Troyens* (The Trojans), taken from the Roman poet Virgil, was finished about 1860 but was not performed for thirty years.

Berlioz's opera *Roméo et Juliette* and the dramatic cantata *La damnation de Faust* (The Damnation of Faust), both were better received. The grandeur of Berlioz's works was not recognized until a century after his death.

FELIX MENDELSSOHN-BARTHOLDY (Hamburg 1809–Leipzig 1847) Born into a wealthy, cultivated family, Mendelssohn's childhood was spent studying in Berlin where he rediscovered German sacred music. At twenty he made his debut in Berlin conducting Bach's *Passion According to St. Matthew*, which had not been performed for many years. After much traveling, Mendelssohn settled in Leipzig, where he conducted orchestras and composed, gaining notice with his famous wedding march in *A Midsummer Night's Dream*. He also wrote oratorios that were reminiscent of Bach and Handel, two symphonies based on religious themes, and concertos and *Lieder*, while his *Italian* and *Scotch* symphonies reflected pleasant memories of his travels.

FRYDERYK CHOPIN (Warsaw 1810–Paris 1849) Chopin, whose father was French and mother was Polish, had a good education at the school in Warsaw, Poland, where his father taught French, as well as a musical education at the Conservatory, so it was as a well-trained musician that he made his piano debut in Vienna in 1829. Chopin left Vienna for London two years later, but he stopped over in Paris and never left. In Paris, as the idol of the artistic and literary world, he knew artists such as the painter Delacroix and writers such as George Sand, whose real name was Amandine Dudevant and with whom Chopin had a long-standing and tempestuous love affair. For his last ten years, Chopin had a serious lung condition that finally took his life.

A melancholy composer, Chopin's compositions are brief and intense, especially the piano *Nocturnes* and *Études*, while nostalgia for his oppressed Polish homeland can be heard in his Polonaises and Mazurkas.

ROBERT SCHUMANN (Zwickau 1810–Bonn 1856) Schumann, whose father was a bookseller and publisher, founded a music journal when he was twenty-four. While at Leipzig University, where he was a student of Friedrich Wieck, Schumann heard a Paganini concert and decided to leave his law studies to devote himself to music. He married Clara Wieck over Maestro Wieck's great opposition, which even included taking Schumann to court. By then Schumann had composed several works, such as the *Papillons* and the *Intermezzi* for the piano, although few of them had been published. He now began to show signs of mental instability.

In Dresden, Schumann finished the Second Symphony and the Concerto for Orchestra with Clara at the piano. They were coldly received in Prague. More appreciated by the artistic world than by the public, Schumann became director of concerts in Düsseldorf, where he composed the Concerto for Violoncello and Orchestra and his last two symphonies. With his mental illness growing worse, Schumann went to Holland for a rest. Both his friend, the young Johannes Brahms, and Clara were with him when he died in an asylum near Bonn.

RICHARD WAGNER (Leipzig 1813–Venice 1883) Richard Wagner, the creator of the music drama, was an astounding genius who wrote the librettos for all of his music. He was born into a family for which the theater was an essential part of life. Wagner's first major opera was *Rienzi*, set in medieval Rome. Turning to German subjects, Wagner wrote his two early masterpieces, *The Flying Dutchman* and *Tannhäuser*. A political activist, he had to flee from the German police in 1849 and make a new life for himself in Switzerland. His tragedy *Lohengrin* had to wait years before Liszt performed it in Weimar. Meanwhile Wagner was slowly completing his gigantic four-opera epic, *The Ring of the Nibelungen*. In 1864 the unhappy and impoverished composer was invited to Munich by King Louis II, and eventually *Tristan and Isolde* and *Die Meistersinger* (The Master Singers) were performed there. Wagner had a theater built in Bavaria exclusively for his operas, which have been given there almost every year since 1876. Wagner, like Verdi, was a colossus in the world of music.

FRANZ LISZT (Raiding 1811–Bayreuth 1886) Liszt was a composer, pianist, adventurer, the father of Richard Wagner's second wife, and the creator of the symphonic poem. At the age of eight he played the piano for Prince Nikolaus Esterházy, a Hungarian nobleman, and was soon famous. With money donated by several Hungarian aristocrats, he went to Vienna to study, where he met Beethoven. He then made concert tours throughout Europe. In 1848 he was court *Kapellmeister* (musical director/conductor) in Weimar, Germany, where he performed Wagner's *Lohengrin* for the first time. He organized a Berlioz festival and composed twelve symphonic poems and two symphonies—the *Faust Symphony*, inspired by Goethe's poem, and the *Dante Symphony*, based on the *Divine Comedy*. In 1859 he took holy orders—the Pope made him the Abbé Liszt. In the summer of 1886 he went to Bayreuth for a Wagnerian festival, caught a cold, and died. Liszt has been called "the Paganani of the Piano" as well as "the founder of modern music."

GUISEPPE VERDI (Busseto 1813–Milan 1901) Even though he studied under the town organist, Verdi was not admitted to the Milan Conservatory, but nonetheless he made a successful debut at Milan's La Scala Opera House with *Oberto conte di San Bonifacio* (Oberto, Count of San Bonifacio). With the triumph of the heroic *Nabucco* in 1842, and *I Lombardi alla prima crociata* (The Lombards on the First Crusade) in 1843, Verdi's career was launched. In the next five years he wrote *Ernani; Attila,* based on the story of Attila the Hun; *I masnadieri* (The Robbers), and the delicate love story *Luisa Miller.* These were followed by the ever-popular *Rigoletto, Il trovatore* (The Troubadour), and *La traviata* (The Fallen Woman). He wrote *I vespri siciliani* (The Sicilian Vespers) in 1855, followed by *Un ballo in maschera* (The Masked Ball), *La forza del destino* (The Force of Destiny), *Don Carlos,* and *Aida.*

Verdi then retired to his estate, a wealthy and world-famous man. There he composed the *Requiem Mass,* and his only comic opera, *Falstaff,* the crowning achievement of a long life of creativity.

Verdi, like Wagner, was during his growth a politically committed composer. His works, like Wagner's, will always be performed.

CHARLES GOUNOD (Paris 1818–Saint-Cloud 1893) Gounod, who studied at the conservatory of Paris, won the Prix de Rome, after which he spent three years in Rome where, attracted to traditional Catholic music, he wrote masses and a requiem. He then dedicated himself to opera, achieving European fame with *Faust.* Although Gounod lived most of his life in Paris, he spent some years in London, where he composed a number of oratorios, twelve masses, and another *Requiem.*

JACQUES OFFENBACH (Cologne 1819–Paris 1880) The son of a cantor, Offenbach left home when very young. He settled in Paris, where he played the violoncello for a living, then became manager of the Bouffes-Parisiens theater and of the Gaîté theater, at the same time composing operettas. He wrote ninety-five of these, some of which helped make him wealthy and famous and some of which were failures. His only "serious" opera was *Les Contes d'Hoffmann* (The Tales of Hoffmann), which is still performed throughout the world. Offenbach captured the witty, satirical spirit of his beloved Paris.

BEDŘICH SMETANA (Litomyšl 1824–Prague 1884) Smetana, who grew up in a musical family, began to compose while very young. He was also interested in Bohemian (Czechoslovakian) musical traditions. In 1861 he helped to found an opera house in Prague. It was there that he put on some of his own operas, including the famous *Prodaná nevěsta* (The Bartered Bride), which is still very popular. His cycle of symphonic poems, *My Country,* and his quartet *From My Life,* which is autobiographical and which musically describes the beginning of his mental illness, are frequently performed. Smetana died in an insane asylum.

ALEXANDER PORFIREVICH BORODIN (St. Petersburg 1833–1887) Because he was an illegitimate child, Borodin was given the name of one of his father's serfs (slaves). His mother made him study medicine despite his obvious musical talents. While a doctor in the Russian Army, Borodin met Mussorgsky. Together with Balakirev, Cui, and Rimsky-Korsakov, they founded the Group of Five, which revolutionized Russian music, giving it Russian themes and settings.

The opera *Prince Igor* is Borodin's most famous work. It is filled with drama and colorful folklore. The orchestral composition *In the Steppes of Central Asia* is frequently played today. Borodin was also a scientist who taught organic chemistry at the Military Academy in St. Petersburg, and made important discoveries in that field.

JOHANNES BRAHMS (Hamburg 1833–Vienna 1897) Brahms received early musical instruction from his father, and as a young man had to earn his living by playing the piano in low taverns on the Hamburg waterfront. Gaining fame as a pianist, he got to know Liszt and Schumann, and was only twenty when Schumann wrote an article about him in his journal that attracted the attention of the German musical world. After his first piano compositions, Brahms went on to more complex musical forms such as his *German Requiem,* based on Martin Luther's Bible. He also wrote *Lieder,* chamber music, organ music, and piano concertos, but never attempted an opera. His four superb symphonies are standard works for every symphony orchestra, like the symphonies of Beethoven.

GEORGES BIZET (Paris 1838–Bougival 1875) Born into a family of musicians, Bizet studied *solfeggio* (sight-reading) at the age of four and entered the Paris Conservatory at ten. He won the Grand Prix de Rome and wrote his first opera, *Don Procopio,* in Rome, but was unable to have it put on. Any failure depressed him, and with little faith in his talents, he often withdrew works that were already in rehearsal. Critics liked to accuse him of imitating Verdi and Wagner, and treated his *Pêcheurs de perles* (The Pearl Fishers) harshly. Because of a fire, his *Don Rodrigue* could not be performed at the Paris Opéra. When his tragic opera *Carmen,* the story of a Spanish gypsy, was poorly received at its premiere,

Bizet fell sick and died a few days later under mysterious circumstances.

MODEST PETROVICH MUSSORGSKY (Karevo, Pskov 1839– St. Petersburg 1881) Having spent his early childhood among peasants, Mussorgsky came to know the Russian people, folk traditions, and songs. Although his land-owner father made him join the army, one of his piano pieces attracted the attention of the composer Balakirev, who gave him composition lessons and put him in touch with other musicians who also were interested in the musical heritage of the Russian people.

Mussorgsky resigned from the army in 1858 to dedicate himself to music, but was soon in financial difficulty. Alcohol weakened his already-poor health. As his brother's guest in the country, Mussorgsky produced a series of compositions, including *A Night on the Bald Mountain*. Obtaining a position in St. Petersburg and living with family friends, Mussorgsky composed the tragic opera *Boris Godunov*, which was rejected by the Imperial Theater. A second version was presented in 1874 to mixed reviews. Mussorgsky also wrote songs and compositions for piano, the tone poem *Pictures from an Exhibition*, and other operas.

PYOTR ILYICH TCHAIKOVSKY (Votkinsk 1840–St. Petersburg 1893) His father wanted him to study law, but Tchaikovsky pursued a musical career to which his mother had introduced him. He first gave music lessons to support himself. After receiving a prize at the end of his conservatory studies, he taught harmony for ten years, a period of great creativity out of which came the Second and Third Symphonies as well as other compositions. A rich noblewoman who admired Tchaikovsky but whom he never met gave him a salary so that he could dedicate himself entirely to composing. Tchaikovsky then composed the three famous ballets *Swan Lake, Sleeping Beauty,* and the *Nutcracker* and the operas *Eugene Onegin* and *The Queen of Spades.*

ANTONÍN DVOŘÁK (Kralup 1841–Prague 1904) Dvořák's first musical influence was his father and an uncle who sent him to the Prague Organ School. In 1874 he was given a salary that enabled him to devote all his time to composing. He soon made himself internationally known with the *Slavonic Dances* as well as the *Stabat Mater*, which was performed in London in 1881. From 1892 to 1895 Dvořák was director of the New York Conservatory, where he composed his most famous work, *From the New World.* Received triumphantly on his return home, he became director of the Prague Conservatory and also presented works at the National Theater, including the opera *Rusalka.* Among his symphonic-vocal compositions were the *Requiem* and the *Te Deum.*

EDVARD GRIEG (Bergen 1843–1907) Grieg, a Norwegian, was sent by his mother to Leipzig, where he studied German Romantic music, after which he went to Copenhagen, Denmark, where he studied Scandinavian music and culture. Grieg, who toured Europe as a pianist and conductor, included typical Nordic themes in his concerts. He founded a musical society in Oslo, Norway, and organized the first Norwegian music festival in his hometown of Bergen. His best-known works are the *Peer Gynt Suites*, the *Norwegian Songs and Dances*, and the *Lyric Suite.* He wrote over 120 beautiful songs as well as piano, chamber, orchestral, and choral music.

NIKOLAY RIMSKY-KORSAKOV (Novgorod 1844–St. Petersburg 1908) Although Rimsky-Korsakov followed family tradition as a naval officer, he also studied music, becoming a professor of composition at St. Petersburg Conservatory. As a professor and member of the Group of Five, Rimsky-Korsakov helped his companions, as well as spreading the Group's ideas and works throughout Europe. He wrote several operas and important symphonic compositions, among which were *Capriccio Espagnol, Sheherazade,* and the *Russian Easter Overture.* Stravinsky was his pupil.

GIACOMO PUCCINI (Lucca 1858–Brussels 1924) All of Puccini's family, back to his great-great-grandfather, were musicians. In 1875 Giacomo became church organist in a village near Lucca, Italy. He later attended the Milan Conservatory, where he lived an impoverished but carefree "bohemian" life. He first attracted international attention with his opera *Manon Lescaut;* then his most famous opera, *La Bohème,* based on his student days, appeared in 1896. Puccini became a wealthy man and settled in beautiful Torre del Lago, where he wrote the violent political tragedy *Tosca* and *Madama Butterfly.* For the Metropolitan Opera in New York he composed *La Fanciulla del West* (The Girl of the Golden West). After further international successes, Puccini died of throat cancer before completing *Turandot,* an opera set in ancient Cathay (China). Puccini is possibly the world's best-loved opera composer.

ISAAC ALBÉNIZ (Camprodón 1860–Cambo-les-Bains 1909) Isaac Albéniz had a brilliant career as a concert pianist in Europe and America. He continued to study in Leipzig and Brussels and was a pupil of Liszt's at Weimar and in Rome. Albéniz gave successful concerts of his own compositions from 1880 until 1893, when he settled in Paris to concentrate entirely on composing. He composed 250 pieces for the piano, including the suite *Iberia,* the twelve *Piezas caractisticas* (Characteristic Pieces), *Recuerdos de viaje* (Travel Memories), the *Spanish Suite,* and *España,* as well as the opera *Pepita Jiménez.*

GUSTAV MAHLER (Kališt 1860–Vienna 1911) After studying at the Vienna Conservatory, Mahler at twenty began a brilliant career as a conductor, working in the theaters of Prague, Leipzig, Budapest, Hamburg, and finally Vienna, where he directed the Court Opera from 1897 to 1907. Because his symphonies had little success, and because he was severely criticized for his personal interpretation of the music of the past, Mahler left Vienna to accept a position at the Metropolitan Opera in New York, but he stayed for only a year, returning to Vienna in 1911. Mahler died that year.

Mahler alternated incomparable conducting with his creative life, which is expressed well in his nine symphonies, as well as a tenth which remained unfinished, perhaps by choice. He also composed cycles of superb *Lieder*.

CLAUDE DEBUSSY (Saint-Germain-en-Laye 1862–Paris 1918) Debussy entered the Paris Conservatory at the age of ten but left for Rome after winning the Prix de Rome. Returning to Paris, he entered the world of writers and Impressionist painters, and was attracted to both the Russian and Oriental music that he heard at the Universal Exposition of 1889.

Although Debussy's symphonic poem *Prélude à l'après-midi d'un faune* (Prelude to the Afternoon of a Faun), on which he worked for ten years, received mixed reviews, it ultimately became famous, as did his compositions for piano—*Images*, *Préludes*, and *Études*, his sonatas and above all, his symphonic sketch *La mer*. He wrote one opera, *Pelléas et Mélisande*.

RICHARD STRAUSS (Munich 1864–Garmisch 1949) Son of a musician in the Bavarian court orchestra, Richard Strauss showed talent at an early age. He began his career as a conductor before he was twenty in Munich and Berlin under the guidance of Hans von Bülow, the famous Wagnerian conductor. Strauss also made triumphant tours in Europe and America with the Berlin Philharmonic. As director of the Berlin Opera (1908–1918) and the Vienna Opera (1919–1924), he greatly influenced German music. In 1933 he became president of the *Musikkammer* of Hitler's Third Reich, for which he was severely criticized.

Strauss had made his debut as a composer with the symphonic poem *Don Giovanni* in 1894. He then wrote a series of tone poems including *Tod und Verklärung* (Death and Transfiguration), *Also sprach Zarathustra* (Thus Spake Zarathustra), *Don Quixote*, and *Ein Heldenleben* (A Hero's Life). Strauss also composed symphonies, works for instruments and soloists, *Lieder*, and many operas, including *Salome*, which was banned in New York, *Elektra*, and *Die Frau ohne Schatten* (The Woman Without a Shadow). Strauss has been called the successor of Wagner, but his music can stand on its own.

JEAN SIBELIUS (Hämeenlinna 1865–Järvenpää 1957) Sibelius, who was Finnish, began his studies in Helsinki, completing them in Berlin and Vienna. He returned to Finland in 1892 to become professor at the Helsinki Conservatory. In 1904, after Sibelius was awarded a state pension so that he could devote all his time to composing, he retired. He is perhaps best known for seven symphonies inspired by ancient Finnish sagas, but also composed many other kinds of music.

ENRIQUE GRANADOS (Lérida 1867–English Channel 1916) Granados studied in Paris and was soon well known as a pianist, enjoying a long career as a concert pianist. He founded the academy in Barcelona, Spain, that now carries his name. He composed seven musical works for the theater, including the *Goyescas*, which played in New York in 1916. His music for piano was even more important, especially the twelve *Spanish Dances*.

ARNOLD SCHÖNBERG (Vienna 1874–Los Angeles 1951) Schönberg's mother gave him his first music lessons. Needing money, he took a bank job while continuing his musical studies with the help of a friend at the Conservatory. After becoming conductor of a modest workers' choir, Schönberg left the bank to compose full time, making a mark with his string sextet *Verklärte Nacht* (Transfigured Night) and with his first *Lieder*. Both Strauss and Mahler were impressed by Schönberg, but it was Mahler who helped him and who became a lasting friend.

Together with other artists, such as the painters Vasili Kandinski and Franz Marc, Schönberg formed the "Blue Knights," a group that advocated the new art form called Expressionism. During this period Schönberg composed *Erwartung* (Expectation), *Die glückliche Hand* (The Knack), and *Pierrot lunaire* (Moonstruck Pierrot). Schönberg also gathered around him students such as Berg and Webern, forming the "School of Vienna."

After World War I, Schönberg taught composition at the Berlin State Academy, but the Nazis called his music degenerate. A Jew, he emigrated to the United States, where he became a professor of music at the University of California.

MAURICE RAVEL (Ciboure 1875–Paris 1937) Although Ravel was of Basque (Spanish) origin, he lived in Paris, where he studied at the Conservatory. Later he composed some of his most famous works such as the Habanera for Two Pianos and the *Pavane pour une infante défunte* (Pavan for a Dead Infanta). He wrote his Concerto for the Left Hand for a pianist who was mutilated in World War I. Ravel also composed *La Valse* and *Boléro* for ballet, as well as writing sonatas, concertos, and tone poems for voices. His best works were his orchestral compositions, which include the *Rapsodie espagnole* (Spanish Rhapsody) and the orchestration for Mussorgsky's *Pictures at an Exhibition*.

MANUEL DE FALLA (Cádiz 1876–Cordoba, Argentina 1946) Educated musically by his mother, de Falla went to Madrid to study when he was ten and from there to Paris. After settling in Paris, de Falla, always drawn to his Spanish homeland, wrote *Nights in the Gardens of Spain* for piano and orchestra, followed by two famous ballets, *El amor brujo* (Love, the Magician) and *El sombrero de tres picos* (The Three-Cornered Hat). De Falla returned to Spain in 1914. In 1939 he went to Argentina, where he died. His art is based on Spanish folk songs.

IGOR FEDOROVICH STRAVINSKY (Oranienbaum 1882–New York 1971) Stravinsky studied music at the university in St. Petersburg, where he was a student of Rimsky-Korsakov's. In 1908 he began working with Diaghilev, the director of the *Ballets-Russes* in Paris, producing *The Firebird* in 1910 and *Petrouchka* in 1911, both of which brought Stravinsky immediate fame, although his controversial *The Rite of Spring* (1913) scandalized the artistic world.

During World War I, Stravinsky lived in Switzerland, returning to Paris when the war was over. Meanwhile, he had written the stage play *L'histoire du soldat* (A Soldier's Story), ballets, concertos, and oratorios produced in rapid succession. In his "neoclassical" period he wrote works such as *Oedipus Rex*, *Apollon Musagète*, and the opera *The Rake's Progress*. When World War II broke out, Stravinsky was in the United States, and in 1945 he became an American citizen. Although he died in New York, his wish was to be buried in Venice.

ANTON VON WEBERN (Vienna 1883–Salzburg 1945) Webern earned a degree in musicology from the University of Vienna, after which he became Schönberg's student. With the 6 Orchestral Pieces (1913), Webern was already on the road to composing what was called dodecaphonic (twelve-note) music. His *Lieder* and other compositions were ignored as too "unmusical" by the public. Despite these setbacks, as well as financial difficulties, Webern wrote the *Trio* in 1927 and the *Symphony* in 1928, in which his personal style emerged.

In 1927 Webern worked for the Vienna radio, but the Nazis dismissed him in 1934 and censored his music. Withdrawing into the mountains near Salzburg, Webern was mistakenly shot by an American soldier at the end of World War II.

ALBAN BERG (Vienna 1885–1935) Berg, who began as an amateur pianist, became a student and lifelong friend of Schönberg's, the two men sharing theories and joining in their search for new forms of musical expression. Berg was a soldier in World War I. His music was forbidden during the Nazi regime.

His first compositions, under Schönberg's influence, were *Lieder*, the Sonata for Piano, and the String Quartet. His first great operatic work was *Wozzeck* (premiered in 1925). His other operatic masterpiece, the "atonal" *Lulu*, was only recently completed by another composer.

GEORGE GERSHWIN (New York 1898–Hollywood 1937) Gershwin grew up in Brooklyn, learning songs and studying music in a rather lighthearted way, but after starting work at a music publisher, he began composing. His song "Swanee," sung by Al Jolson in 1919, was a hit, and Gershwin was asked to write for Broadway shows. Encouraged by Paul Whiteman, Gershwin wrote *Rhapsody in Blue* for piano and orchestra. It was first performed in 1924 by Whiteman. Gershwin continued writing this type of jazz symphony with such compositions as the Concerto in F, *An American in Paris*, and the Cuban Overture.

EDWARD "DUKE" ELLINGTON (Washington 1899–New York 1974) Duke Ellington began to study the piano at seven and played in local orchestras as a boy. He formed the group "Washingtonians" in 1923 and made his first record in 1925. In 1926 he enlarged his band, which soon became one of the most important big bands in America. In 1937 Duke made a series of concert tours and performed nearly every year in New York's Carnegie Hall. He wrote over nine hundred compositions, including "Solitude," "Sophisticated Lady," and "Creole Love Call."

LOUIS "SATCHMO" ARMSTRONG (New Orleans 1900–New York 1971) Armstrong, who came from a poor family, had already been in a reformatory at age thirteen, where he had begun to play the cornet, switching later to the trumpet. At eighteen he made his debut in the band of Kid Ory as a substitute. In 1919 he played on the Mississippi riverboats, making his first record with the Creole Jazz Band of King Oliver in Chicago and founding the "Hot Five," which later became the "Hot Seven," in 1925.

Because of his personality, origins, and musical gifts, Armstrong soon became representative of all jazz music. He went to England in 1932 on tour, making an extensive European tour two years later. After World War II, he and his band triumphantly toured the world as a symbol of jazz.

BENNY (BENJAMIN) GOODMAN (Chicago 1909–New York 1986) Goodman, who came from a modest family, began to study the clarinet in a synagogue school at the age of ten. After further study, he played in a dance orchestra, making his first record in 1926 with Ben Pollock's orchestra. In 1936, after years of working in shows and on radio, Benny Goodman, called The King of Swing, formed his own band, bringing together the best jazz musicians. He also was a classical clarinetist and appeared with the New York Philharmonic.

BENJAMIN BRITTEN (Lowestoft 1913–Aldeburgh 1976) Primarily a vocal composer, Britten was a child prodigy whose early works such as the *Sinfonietta* and *A Simple Symphony* have become very popular. His first triumph was the opera *Peter Grimes* (1945), which was followed by many other works for the musical theater including *The Turn of the Screw* and *Billy Budd*. He wrote a *War Requiem* in 1962 and two works for children, *The Little Chimneysweep* and *Noyes Fluddes*, as well as church parables, concertos, choral works, songs, and works for films.

THE BEATLES. The Beatles were a vocal and instrumental group consisting of John Lennon, Paul McCartney, George Harrison, and Ringo Starr, all born in Liverpool between 1940 and 1943. The Beatles made their first record in 1962, and their music, which was almost immediately mythologized by American and European youth, symbolized the so-called "beat" music (a fusion of American blues, rock, and European folk songs), with "Yesterday," "Michelle," "Yellow Submarine," "Let It Be," and "Imagine," among their most notable songs.

In 1970 the group broke up, with each member continuing independently as musician or singer. Paul McCartney and George Harrison are still active in the record business. John Lennon was murdered in New York in 1980.

Index of Names